Angels of the Swamp

Walker's American History Series
for Young People

WALKER'S AMERICAN HISTORY SERIES
FOR YOUNG PEOPLE

Angels of the Swamp

DOROTHY RAYMOND WHITTAKER

Walker and Company
New York

THIS BOOK WAS EDITED BY FRAN NANKIN

First published in the United States of America in 1992
by Walker Publishing Company, Inc.

Published simultaneously in Canada by Thomas Allen & Son
Canada, Limited, Markham, Ontario

Library of Congress Cataloging-in-Publication Data
Whittaker, Dorothy Raymond.
Angels of the swamp / Dorothy Raymond Whittaker.
p.   cm.—(Walker's American history series for young people)
Summary: Taffy, a fifteen-year-old orphan, joins two boys who have
been forced to leave their homes and the three of them try to
survive the summer of 1932 on an island off the west coast of
Florida.
ISBN 0-8027-8129-2
[1. Florida—Fiction.   2. Depressions—1929—
Fiction.   3. Orphans—
Fiction.]   I. Title.   II. Series.
PZ7.W6173An   1991
[Fic]—dc20   91-19692
CIP
AC

Jacket author photo by Bruce Montgomery

Printed in the United States of America

2   4   6   8   10   9   7   5   3   1

ACKNOWLEDGMENTS

Special thanks to my friends the late author Wyatt Blassingame and his wife, Jeanne, whose avid interest in the writing of my novel inspired me to continue on to the end.

Thanks also for the encouragement I received from my family and friends, especially Virginia Schneck Caton, who read and edited my revised copies no less than a dozen times.

Betty Jo Anderson is also included in my acknowledgments for her loyalty and patience in the typing of my manuscript.

This book is dedicated to my father, who provided me, in my growing up years, with a wealth of knowledge pertaining to nature and the fascinating creatures of the sea.

AUTHOR'S NOTE

The story you are about to read is based largely on experiences I had as a child. I grew up on Anna Maria, a small island on Florida's west coast, during the Great Depression. My family lived in a houseboat until I was twelve years old, and I considered the waters of Tampa Bay my backyard.

During the summers, my brother and I plodded the pristine grass flats in the backwaters of Tampa Bay harvesting shellfish at low tide. We sold our catch daily, riding our bicycles to the village at the north end of the island to make deliveries. Mostly, we caught scallops because everyone wanted them. We learned to open them properly and sold the small white muscles for fifty cents a quart. We also caught clams and blue crabs.

It has been said that the fishermen and the farmers fared better than most during the Depression years because they usually had food on the table. In some ways, we found this to be true, though, with money being so tight, we had our problems, too. In any event, the most widely used medium of exchange in those days was bartering, not hard cash.

We had no competition selling the shellfish because most of the other youngsters on the island didn't have the easy access to the back bay waters that we had. Or they were reluctant to put their feet into the water, where the dreaded stingrays were prevalent. All during the time my brother and I traipsed through the grass flats, neither of us ever got stung. We had learned early on how to identify the half-buried creatures, and we knew to be cautious at all times. Avoiding the stingrays became as natural to us as breathing.

The shellfishing we did made an important contribution to our family income, though it hardly seemed like work to us. Our mother put aside the money we earned and doled out only enough for one small ice cream cone each during our deliveries. The rest of the money went toward our visits to the dentist and school clothes in the fall.

My brother and I felt fortunate to be able to contribute in the way that we did. It made us feel important—part of a solution to our problems. If nothing else, the Great Depression brought families like ours closer together.

—D.R.W., HOLMES BEACH, FLORIDA, 1991

Angels of the Swamp

≈ 1 ≈

Taffy stood barefoot on the port side of the skiff with a long, slender poling oar balanced in her hands. Her face was flushed. Perspiration glistened over her body. With one foot propped on the railing of the boat, she scanned the boundaries of Little Placid Bay stretching out like polished glass. A warm Florida sun poured over the maze of small islands dotting the water as far as she could see. Except for a channel marker in the distance, all traces of civilization had vanished.

In the center of the boat, a tarpaulin covered an assortment of gear, leaving just enough legroom for easy poling from either side. Seated on the head cap was a black tomcat. With small darting motions of his head, he watched a pair of cormorants cavorting off the bow.

Taffy sat down on the stern seat and drew a long, ragged breath. She had been poling at a steady pace for two hours; the fishing village was now far behind her. She wanted to rest, but she could not feel at ease until she was well inside the big swamp known as Cranes Bog. Only then, hidden away from the outside world, would she know she was finally safe from Miss Bessie Tyler.

The thought of Miss Bessie, the welfare agent, brought Taffy to her feet. She picked up the poling oar and shoved hard, her shoulders aching. She was tired to the bone, but her fatigue had not been brought on by the poling. At age fifteen, she was used to that. It was the past three days that had taken their toll on her body. Her grandfather's sudden death. Miss Bessie trying to put Taffy into a foster home. Her sudden decision to get away.

Even the nights had not been her own; nightmares about her grandfather robbed her of sleep. Loneliness clung to her like a sickness, like a hard rock in the pit of her stomach. It was there now.

Only this morning her grandfather had been laid to rest in the cemetery on the outskirts of Bayview. Taffy had sat through the service, knowing that nothing would ever be the same again.

Then, when she had set out in the skiff, thinking only of slipping away undetected, she had made the mistake of looking back. There, standing on stilts over the water, was the weathered little fishing shack with the sheet metal roof blazing in the sun. Two rainwater barrels stood on the deck. Taffy had still been able to see the potted geraniums, splotches of red on the back porch.

Pangs of homesickness had bitten deep into her insides. This was the home where she had lived with her grandfather, Dandy. She had turned away abruptly, and not looked back again.

≈

The sun was high in the western sky when Taffy left Little Placid Bay and came into the body of water called Big Placid Bay. A breeze rippled the surface of the water. She angled her straw hat down over her eyes and studied the area ahead. The swamp, she remembered, was on the north side of the bay. Its outer shoreline looked like all other shorelines, so its entrances usually went undetected except to the trained eye. Taffy estimated the distance to the first entrance to be only minutes away.

Excitement rippled through her.

She poled on, thinking about Cranes Bog, a seemingly

endless network of jungle islands and hidden lagoons. A place where few people ventured, it was said to be infested with insects and snakes. A time-forgotten region where one could easily get lost and wander around for days before finding one of the four exits to the outside world.

There was nothing formidable about Cranes Bog to Taffy. To show her what the swamp was like, her grandfather had taken her there several times. He had explained why it was so easy to get lost. Inside, he told her, the odd-shaped islands lay parallel to one another and soon blocked the exits from view. But no matter where she was, if she set a course due south, winding around in back of the islands as she came to them, sooner or later she would come to one of the exits.

To Taffy, those trips into Cranes Bog had been fascinating experiences. The big swamp was a primitive place. Mysterious. Intriguing.

≈

Taffy poled on, careful to watch the shoreline ahead.

And then she saw the smooth arc of the white sandbar curving out from shore. Her heartbeat quickened. One of the entrances to the swamp!

After she had entered, all traces of the west wind died, holding the area in a grip of strange, deep silence. The enormity of Cranes Bog was breathtaking. Small green islands mingled with open waters. Mullet rippled the surface. Stingarees slid over the grassy bottom as the boat drifted on. When Taffy looked back, the opening already had disappeared from view.

Relief flooded through her. She was safe. No one would find her now. Relaxation brought an unexpected weakness to her body. She shoved the blade end of the poling oar under the bow and sat down. Drowsiness came over her. She dropped the anchor over the side of the boat. Strain and stress had taken their toll. She curled up on the stern seat. Within seconds, she fell asleep.

≈

A half hour later, Taffy woke up sobbing. She had been dreaming. She was at the cemetery again, just as she had been that morning, except in the dream she sobbed with abandon all through the service. This time, it did not seem important that she was making a spectacle of herself. Feelings of loneliness and despair were more than she could bear.

In the dream, she saw the raw ugliness of the graveyard. Dead leaves fluttered in the breeze, catching at the edges of the tombstones. She saw the still face in the pine box and felt her heart breaking. And she heard the words of Reverend Hammond: ". . . In my Father's house are many mansions. . . . I go to prepare a place. . . ."

In the dream, she petitioned God all over again. Her grandfather was a simple man. Taffy was sure he wouldn't care very much about a mansion. So please, God, she prayed, let him have a small place by the sea, a place like the one he had here on Earth.

In the dream, Mr. Tanner, her grandfather's lifelong friend, was beside her. The old man reached out to comfort her, holding her close while she wept, but, in her terrible state of distress, she had been beyond solace.

And that was how Taffy felt when she woke up. Beyond solace.

She sat up slowly, brushing away the tears. She leaned over the side of the skiff and splashed cool salt water over her face.

The simple act brought her back to reality. She looked around. Patches of green seaweed floated by. The tide was coming in. She rose to her feet and tested her legs. The weakness was gone. She picked up the poling oar, gently nudging the skiff. There was no need to hurry anymore. But there were things she had to do.

All afternoon she had watched a band of low-lying clouds making up on the western horizon. It was April. A front could still come blowing in, bringing rain. Somewhere in the swamp she would find a narrow stream running through one of the mangrove islands. She would drape the tarpaulin over the branches and make camp for the night.

But first she had to find such a place.

As she poled on, watchful for a gap in the mangroves, her thoughts turned to the welfare agent. Miss Bessie was scheduled to pick up Taffy tomorrow morning to take her to her new home in the country. Foster parents. The pig farm. Taffy was to be ready to leave at eight o'clock sharp.

Taffy grinned. At eight o'clock tomorrow morning, Miss Bessie was going to be in for a surprise.

As far back as Taffy could remember, Miss Bessie had tried to take her from her grandfather's home in Buttonwood Harbor. The woman wanted to place her in a foster home fifteen miles away, in Bayview. Cap't. Hansen was too old to take care of his granddaughter, she had charged repeatedly. He had made no attempt to provide her with a proper home. Worse still, he had forced child labor on the girl, using her on the launch to help with the nets.

But of course nothing had ever come of her efforts, except to make an enemy of Taffy's grandfather and stir up the entire community of Buttonwood Harbor, including her husband, Cap't. Nate. None of it, however, had deterred Miss Bessie.

"You're not going to get your way this time either, Miss Bessie," Taffy said out loud. She remembered the cruel and disrespectful manner in which Miss Bessie had presented her ultimatum to Taffy. It was the day her grandfather had died.

Taffy had been alone in the shack, when, unannounced, the welfare agent had pushed the screen door open and barged in.

"My dear Taffy, I'm so sorry . . ."

Miss Bessie's eyes darted around the small room, taking in everything. The unfinished cast net hanging in the center of the room. The bits of paper stuffed in the holes in the screen. Cracks in the rough flooring wide enough to see the water below. The rust spots in the tin roof.

Although Taffy had been in shock, she had known Miss Bessie wasn't sorry at all.

The welfare agent had been wearing her usual plastered smile. "We must talk about your future, child. . . ."

Taffy had stared at the woman, not understanding her meaning. Her grandfather had just died. All she could think about was her grandfather.

Miss Bessie had rambled on, something about people who could converse on subjects other than the price of fish. "I have a place in mind, my dear. . . ."

Taffy remembered sitting very still, feeling the blood drain from her face. This she understood. Miss Bessie was trying once more to send her away!

By the time Miss Bessie had left, Taffy had been in a panic.

Foster home! How she hated those two words that still had the power to stir up frightening memories of the dark past, before she had come to live with her grandfather. She had had enough of foster homes.

But this time, with her grandfather gone, there was nothing to stop Miss Bessie, unless . . .

To leave home had been a hard decision to make. But there was no other way. Even if there had been a family in the village willing to take Taffy in for a year or two, Miss Bessie would surely have vetoed it. Everyone in the village was too poor, or they weren't proper Christians. The list of complaints would have gone on and on.

Taffy was well aware of the Depression that already had taken its toll on the Deep South. The year was nineteen thirty-two. Besides that, Buttonwood Harbor fishermen were often kept inshore for a week or more at a time during the winter because of bad weather. The price of fish had dropped to practically nothing. So who needed another mouth to feed?

Taffy didn't need someone to look after her anyway. She could take care of herself. Her grandfather had taught her well.

≈ 2 ≈

Jody Hillard jerked his poling oar out of the water and let it drop to the bottom of the boat with a clatter. Here he was, he thought irritably, only two hours out on the water, and already his leg was killing him. He sat on the stern seat and began to unwind a dingy white bandage covering a portion of his lower leg. *Why* was the dang thing having to act up now?

He knew the answer well enough. It was because he hadn't soaked it in hot water and permanganate this morning. Jody was expected, according to the doctor's instructions, to soak his leg twice a day. This morning was the first time in weeks he had slipped up. And now the throbbing ache was back. Infection had built up.

Well, he would just have to put up with it awhile longer, he told himself. Later in the day he would find a suitable island somewhere, one with a bare shoreline, and make camp. Build a fire. Heat some water.

He lifted the bandage to look at a patch of angry red flesh. Pus seeped out of an open wound that was about as big as a quarter.

"Cripes," he muttered.

He reached in his pocket and brought out a bottle of peroxide. He unscrewed the cap and poured directly into the raw place. A froth of yellow bubbles erupted. He watched the liquid spew over and dribble down his leg.

What he needed right now was to get off his leg for a

while. Give it a rest. But he sure wasn't going to sit out here in the middle of Little Placid Bay with the hot sun on his head. He would stop at the next mangrove island he came to and hole up under the overhanging branches.

He washed the bandage overboard, spread it out to dry, then picked up the poling oar and shoved off.

As he poled on, he fumed again about the events that had taken place the night before: his reason for neglecting his leg this morning. It was all his uncle's fault.

Before going to bed last night, Jody had carefully groomed himself. He had wanted to look presentable when he went to the graveside service this morning to pay his respects to Cap't. Hansen. He had scrubbed himself clean, washed the grime out of his hair, even cleaned the dirt out from under his fingernails. The nice clothes he had borrowed from Tuffy Tyson were neatly folded over a chair beside his cot. Jody had gone to bed early so he would be up in plenty of time to soak his leg before getting dressed, but sometime during the night his Uncle John, in his usual fashion, had stumbled in drunk. Instead of falling into bed and passing out like he did every night, he had sat on the floor crooning songs to Jesus that he made up as he went along. Then, later in the night, he'd started in with those awful howling noises, carrying on like he used to do at the revival meetings in the Holy Roller church when the hand of the Almighty was on him.

Nobody could sleep through all that, Jody snorted to himself. He had been kept awake half the night and, as a result, had overslept. There had been no time to soak his leg.

≈

When Jody came to one of the small green islands, he shoved his skiff all the way under the mangrove branches

9

and laid his pole aside. He sat down, easing his leg overboard into clear, cool water. The water seeped soothingly into his wound. With an orange in his hand, he sprawled out on the stern seat and closed his eyes, cursing himself for the hundredth time for allowing the accident to his leg to have happened in the first place. Just plain stupidity, he told himself, and all because of a sorry catfish! That miserable, slimy excuse of a fish!

It had happened three weeks ago, out in the bay when Jody had been trout fishing. Because he didn't have a kicker—an outboard motor—to get him out to the best grounds, he had to fish closer inshore, where he seldom caught trout big enough to keep. But that time had been different. He had caught keepers every time he threw out, bringing in one after another. He had been filling his fish box, all the time thinking about the money the trout would bring in at Mr. Tanner's fish house. Jody remembered the excitement of that day! He hadn't even thought about catfish. As a rule, they never went after the bait as long as other fish were hitting. But that time, the action had still been going on when the unexpected catfish had come sailing into the boat on the end of the line. The dorsal fin had caught Jody in the leg and stuck there, with the catfish struggling to get free. Even before he could ease his hand up under the other two fins to get a good grip, he had started feeling sick. Sweat had broken out over his body. A strange ringing started in his ears.

With great effort, Jody had yanked the fish free. Blood had streamed down his leg, forming a puddle at his feet. He'd dipped his hands over the side, splashing water over his face. Somehow he made it back to the fish house.

The place had been deserted except for Jonas, Mr. Tanner's handy man. He had bandaged Jody's leg and driven him into town to a doctor.

"Particles of fin broken off . . . ," the physician had grunted as he probed. He'd given Jody a shot in the rump and instructions about the care of his leg: White pills three times a day, regular hot water soakings with permanganate crystals, peroxide in the open wound every day.

The doctor had taken off his glasses. He'd looked up at Jonas.

"You the boy's father?"

"No, sir. I'm Jonas Turner, a friend. I was at the docks when the kid came in. He lives with his uncle."

The doctor had put his glasses back on.

"Nasty wound. I may have gotten all the fin out, but I can't be sure. There could be trouble. If the boy's leg doesn't heal properly, see that someone brings him back here."

"Yes, sir."

By then Jody had been feeling uncomfortable. He'd squirmed around on the table where he had been sitting and looked out the window. He had known it was time to pay the bill, and, because Jonas had brought him in, Jonas would be expected to pay. And if Jonas paid, he would never get his money back from Uncle John.

This had been the worst part, Jody remembered. As always, when he needed his uncle, the man didn't come through. It was always Miss Daisy and Mr. Garvin, the two people he sometimes did odd jobs for, who took care of his needs. Miss Daisy bought his school clothes, and Mr. Garvin took him to the dentist with his own kids. Uncle John never did any of these things for Jody.

Jonas had spoken up. "You can make the bill out to me, Doc, and while you're figuring it up, I'll go out to the truck. Got some fresh pompano. All boned out. Figured you might like a mess."

This kind of payment was not new to the doctor. Ever since the Depression had set in, he had been offered everything from plucked chickens to potted houseplants in exchange for his services. But never the highly prized pompano. He'd beamed from ear to ear.

"By all means, son, bring them in."

≈

Jody had felt better after he left the doctor's office with Jonas, but the next morning, when he'd gotten out of bed, his leg had been so sore he couldn't put his weight on it. He could only move about the one-room, palmetto-thatched hut by holding on to furniture. He had needed hot water to begin the soakings, but there had been no water in the house. He had looked around. His uncle's dirty clothes were strewn across the floor. Flies buzzed around empty wine bottles scattered about. Unwillingly, Jody had cast his eyes to the corner bed where his uncle lay sleeping. Dingy bedding covered the man's body to his waist. A week's growth of whiskers bristled over his face. Jody had looked in disgust at the open mouth, lips blowing out foul air with noisy, rhythmic breathing.

As he'd watched, the form on the bed had stirred. Bloodshot eyes had opened, squinting in the bright sunlight. Then Uncle John had sat up and slowly turned unfocused eyes in Jody's direction.

"I've been hurt bad, Uncle John," Jody had said pleadingly. "I can't walk. Get dizzy when I stand up. The doctor said I had to soak my leg in hot water. Please, Uncle John, there's no water in the house. . . ."

Uncle John had stared at Jody, then slowly turned his attention to an empty wine bottle lying on the floor. With shaking hands, he'd picked it up, looking at it mournfully before dropping it back on the floor. He'd groped for his clothes. Somehow he had gotten into them.

"Gotta get down to the docks," he had mumbled. "Gotta go find old Hank. Gotta go back to fishin'."

He had picked up his hat and stumbled to the door.

"Please, Uncle John," Jody had screamed. "Please help me!"

For an instant his uncle hesitated, Jody remembered, but he hadn't looked back.

"Gotta go. . . ." The screen door had slammed behind him.

Jody had cried then. He knew his uncle was not going to the docks to hunt up Cap't. Hank. He was going to Gus's tavern, where a jug of stale spirits would be waiting for him. It didn't matter to Uncle John that the mixture of alcohol in the jug was the beer and wine left in the glasses by Gus's customers during the course of a day's business.

The tavern owner received nothing in return for this service other than the satisfaction of knowing that the hopeless village drunk would be less likely to go haywire some moonlit night and break into his tavern and help himself.

Even so, there were times Uncle John drank more than Gus could provide. He would run up a tab that Gus wasn't very happy about, and Gus would cut him off. Uncle John would go back fishing until his bill was paid, then start in all over again.

And that was the way it had been for the past three years, Jody thought. His uncle just couldn't be bothered with him.

Something had snapped in Jody's mind that morning three weeks ago. He had wiped his tears away and realized that he was finished with the humiliation of living with an alcoholic. Jody was sick of living in a pigsty, ashamed of being known as John Hillard's nephew. It was time for a change. Time to get away.

Things would have been critical for Jody after that had it not been for Miss Daisy Tolliver. She had heard about his mishap and come by the shack every day to help him with his leg until he was able to take care of himself. She had hauled in water, heated it, seen to his pills, and brought in food.

With constant soakings, the soreness in Jody's leg had begun to ease up. He could walk on it for an hour at a time without pain, and as the days wore on he'd found himself doing more and more. While he'd waited for the time when he could leave, he had loaded provisions in his skiff, which was nosed up in a narrow slough in back of his home. He had felt new stirrings of freedom inside him, like a great burden had been lifted from his shoulders. He could hardly wait!

Under the mangroves, Jody pulled his leg out of the water and inspected the injury carefully. He thought about Miss Daisy, who would surely think Jody had lost his mind to be leaving home with his leg in this condition. But never mind, he thought. With proper care, he would be all right.

He made a peanut butter sandwich and chewed it slowly, thinking. He had no immediate plans. He didn't need any. He would just travel, resting when he was tired, catching fish and cooking them over a fire when he was hungry. He would sleep in his tent at night and travel a little each day. When his leg got better and he felt like it, maybe he would catch fish to sell in a fish house farther up the coast. Other than that, he would just take things as they came.

This was not the first time Jody had left home. He had done so many times, for weeks on end, sometimes even months. Although he was only twelve years old, no one had ever seemed to worry about his disappearances. Somewhere along the way, Jody had earned a reputation for being able to take care of himself.

In his travels, he had come to know the waters for miles around. He knew where to find fresh water. He knew the freedoms as well as the dangers of life in the wild. He had little to worry about.

He stretched out on the seat again, dangling his leg overboard. Contentment settled over him. His leg felt better. Before long he would shove off again.

It was while he was in this position that he became aware of sea gulls screaming in the distance. He raised himself on one elbow and peered through the branches, then sat bolt upright. A skiff was up ahead. Someone wearing khakis and a straw hat stood in the stern. As Jody watched, a movement on the head cap caught his eye. A small animal had leaped to the bottom of the boat and reappeared again at the stern seat.

It was a coal black cat.

At the same time, the lone figure took off the straw hat and tossed it on the stern seat. A spill of long, wavy hair, the color of corn silk, tumbled down.

Jody's mouth went dry. *The only hair he had ever seen like that belonged to Miss Taffy Hansen!*

At that moment, Jody couldn't believe what he was seeing. Miss Taffy? Out here, miles from home? Alone? *What was going on?*

As he stared, he saw her pick up her poling oar and move on, heading west. The same direction he was going. Away from home.

He tried to understand this strange new development. With the gear piled up in her boat, it looked as though she might be leaving home. *But why?* Why would she do that?

Only this morning he had seen her at her grandfather's funeral service in Bayview. In fact, he had been directly behind her when she and Mr. Tanner took their seats.

Jody watched Miss Taffy's skiff move on until he lost sight of her behind a small island. Then he scrambled to his knees, hastily pulling at branches until his skiff was out in open water. He picked up his poling oar.

15

What were Miss Taffy's intentions? He was determined to find out. He would follow her, undetected, until he could learn more. At this point, Jody wasn't sure Miss Taffy would appreciate having company. Not his, in any case, Jody deliberated.

Jody's and Miss Taffy's worlds were wide apart. Miss Taffy was in the tenth grade, in high school. Jody was still in grade school. He was lagging behind because of his many absences. Besides that, Miss Taffy and her grandfather hadn't lived in the village as Jody had. Their place was down the shoreline a distance from the main part of the community, and, for that reason, their paths seldom crossed. Miss Taffy was scarcely aware of his existence, Jody thought wistfully, but he had always been very much aware of her.

As he poled on, keeping a sharp lookout for the skiff, he thought back to the first time he had seen her and her grandfather on their fishing launch. Jody had been down at Mr. Tanner's fish house when they were coming in with a load of fish.

As a rule, Jody spent little time hanging around the docks. He was too busy scrounging up jobs for grub money. Jobs like cleaning Miss Daisy's duck pens or pulling weeds in Mr. Garvin's vegetable garden. This time he had gone to the docks to get a mess of mullet for his supper. Mr. Tanner gave Jody mullet any time he wanted them, at no cost, as long as Jody dressed them himself. It was while he was scaling his fish that he had seen the Hansen launch coming in. Cap't. Hansen's big frame had towered above the wheel where he stood, and Miss Taffy, perhaps eleven years old at the time, had sat Indian fashion on the head cap. Jody had heard their cheerful voices drifting over the water even before the boat rounded the last channel marker. When it had pulled up alongside the loading platform, Jody had stared, fascinated. The girl's hair had been caught up at the nape of her neck with a strand of blue yarn. She wore loose-fitting khakis that were rolled up at the knees. Fish scales clung to the front of her shirt.

Jody smiled, remembering that intriguing scene. Fish piled up in the bottom of the boat. The pretty girl working side by side with her grandfather as they pitched fish onto the platform. That black cat they called Tar Baby perched on the engine box.

After that, Jody had tried to time his jobs so that he could see more of Cap't. Hansen's granddaughter. Miss Taffy's sparkling blue eyes and sunny smile always made him feel good.

As to Cap't. Hansen, Jody had come to regard him with deep respect. He was all brawn and muscle, yet soft-spoken, gentle in his ways. He was always smiling and full of good humor. But the thing about him that had impressed Jody most was the relationship the captain shared with his granddaughter.

Somewhere along the way, Jody remembered, his own thoughts concerning that relationship had begun to chew on him. It was the same kind of relationship he had once shared with his Uncle John.

Jody sighed heavily. Neither he nor Miss Taffy was doing all that great, he told himself. She had just lost her grandfather. Jody's Uncle John had been lost to him for three years.

≈ 3 ≈

Small islands gave way to larger ones as Taffy's skiff moved deeper into the swamp. She poled around sand spits, crimson with fiddler crabs. The shrill cries of water birds pierced the silence of the swamp, and, as the boat moved on, she saw mangrove branches hanging thick with brown pelicans. Sea gulls soared overhead. Majestic white herons stalked the flats, and colonies of spoonbills covered the shallows like a pink mist. The cat, seated on the head cap, was entranced with the show.

Taffy brought the bow of the boat to rest on the edge of a sandbar. Tar Baby leaped ashore and cautiously made his way to higher ground. Sea gulls screamed at him. With ears laid back, he quickly dug a hole.

While the cat was busy on the sandbar, Taffy emptied his box and refilled it with dry sand. When she got back to the boat, something in the shallow water caught her attention. Two small, round holes, side by side, showed prominently on the white bottom. The unmistakable, keyhole-shaped markings of the valve of a clam, right at her feet! She dug her fingers in and brought up a hard-shelled quahog. Others were buried nearby.

When the cat jumped back on the head cap, Taffy had a water pail half full of clams. Although she carried an ample amount of food stock, she knew she would have to forage the waters to supplement the supply if she expected it to last. Pleased with her unexpected findings, she stepped back into the boat and shoved off.

The sun was about two hours from dusk when she spied the gap in the foliage of a good-sized island. She could see there was room enough for the skiff at the mouth of the stream, but, once she started in, she found the stream narrowed. Branches scraped the sides of the boat. Just as she was thinking of backing out, she saw a clearing in the stream ahead. She pressed on and found herself in an area the size of a small room. Foliage, hanging thick overhead, all but obliterated the sun. Tar Baby was uneasy. His eyes grew wider as the semidarkness closed in.

Taffy laid the pole down. She glanced around, making a quick inspection. The branches overhead would tone down a rain, and the limbs were high enough to drape a tarpaulin on. She looked down, where the white bottom reflected through pale green water. Off to one side, a pair of sheepsheads lurked under the mangrove roots, fins barely moving in water approximately four feet deep.

Then she heard an unfamiliar sound in the boat.

Plop . . . plop . . .

The cat growled. Taffy whipped around in time to see two dull green snakes slithering over the gear. They wriggled to the side of the boat and slipped overboard.

The cat's fur bristled. He sniffed the air, whiskers distended.

Plop . . .

Another snake fell on the stern seat, momentarily stunned. Taffy stiffened as she stared at the reptile. With quick movements, it too slithered overboard.

In slow motion she turned her head, lifting her eyes to the branches above. She stood still, barely breathing.

Then she saw them.

At first it was only a small movement, barely detectable. Then another, and another. As her vision adjusted,

19

she saw the branches literally come alive with squirming, writhing motions as hundreds of snakes slowly wound themselves around the branches. Others hung suspended over the water.

"*Oh, no!*" she gasped, barely moving her lips.

Plop . . . plop . . . plop . . . Three more landed in the boat.

"*We have to get out of here!*" Taffy whispered frantically.

She eased her hands around the poling oar, picking it up as though it were made of glass. When the boat moved forward, touching the branches, more snakes showered down. She screamed in terror when one landed on the back of her neck. She wiped furiously at it while panic poured through her.

With great effort, she forced herself to stand very still while she tried to assess the situation. The snakes she had seen so far were harmless, she conceded, but what else was up there? Would the next one to come down in the boat be a heavy-bodied, flat-headed cottonmouth?

She shuddered at the thought.

There were two things she could do. She could jam on the poling oar again and bring more snakes down into the boat, or she could go overboard and pull the boat out.

The thought of the cottonmouth settled it. She didn't want to meet up with one of *those* things in the water. She'd take her chances in the boat.

She gritted her teeth and jammed on the poling oar again. The boat moved forward, wedging itself into the narrow passageway while another dozen or so snakes fell in. In a frenzied attempt to escape, the cat leaped to the railing and lost his footing. He let out a howl as he fell into the water.

Taffy scrambled to the side of the boat and hauled him back in. By then, half the snakes she had seen in the trees were darting around in the water. She shoved on the oar again, hard. The skiff moved farther into the narrow passageway. Then, seconds later, it was in open water on the other side of the island.

When the island was safely behind, Taffy put the poling oar down and sank to the seat. One thought was clear in her mind: Rain or no rain, there would be no more poking around in mangrove islands!

Weakness came over her again. Her hands shook uncontrollably, and her teeth chattered. She was cold. The sun was lower over the tops of the trees now, and, while she sat in the boat trying to get warm, more thoughts troubled her. *Why* were all those snakes wadded up like that in one place? Were they just now coming out of hibernation? Was it their mating season? Or was that simply their normal behavior in Cranes Bog?

Until now, Taffy had thought she knew all there was to know about the habits of water snakes. After all, she had lived around them most of her life. Back at the shack, she had seen them crawling around the prop roots of the mangroves. She had found them curled up in the bottom of her boat, draped around pilings under the dock, or half hidden under logs. Water snakes were a part of life, like raccoons and mosquitoes and water birds. But nothing she had ever encountered during her years around the mangroves could begin to compare with the gory tangle of snakes she had just seen. What else was in Cranes Bog that she didn't know about?

A slow, unbidden fear worked its way into her consciousness. Icy chills crawled up her back. With effort, she tried to reason her fear away. After all, she reminded herself, they were only harmless little water snakes.

She had been spooked because there had been so many of them in one place. As for the cottonmouth, she had only seen two of them in her life. They weren't supposed to be all that crazy about salt water. They usually hung out around freshwater rivers or lakes. Or brackish water, maybe. But not here in the salty waters of Cranes Bog.

The cat had given up trying to lick the water from his rakish-looking fur. Taffy picked him up. She wiped him with the tail of her shirt, then hugged him close.

"It's all right, Tar," she murmured. "Those miserable snakes won't be bothering us anymore."

Taffy set the cat on the stern seat and reluctantly got to her feet. Still shaking, she picked up the poling oar and shoved off. Soon a white sandbar came into view. She nudged the bow to shore, lifted the lid of the stern seat, and pulled out a tattered cotton quilt. Sand flies bit into her scalp. Small squirting sounds came from the clams. She looked, uncaring, at the water in the bottom of the boat. She should be scrounging firewood, putting up a tent. But she was just too tired, too weary. At this point, she didn't care about the jobs staring her in the face. She threw out the anchor, wrapped the quilt tight around her, and, with the cat in her arms, curled up on the stern seat. Sleep came over her quickly.

≈ **4** ≈

Jody squirmed out of his shirt. He dipped it overboard and, without bothering to wring it out, slipped it back on. The cool wetness felt good.

His skiff was snubbed up under the mangroves on an island in Cranes Bog, a safe distance from the sandbar where Miss Taffy had stopped for the night. Jody had concealed himself well. From his position, he could watch Miss Taffy without being seen. Right now, however, there wasn't much to see. Miss Taffy was wrapped in a quilt, resting, and the cat was grooming himself on the head cap.

Jody wasn't sure why he thought it necessary to stay hidden from Miss Taffy, but he had the feeling she wanted to be alone. There were too many unanswered questions for him to barge in just yet. *Why* was she here? *Where* was she going?

However it was, Jody had been greatly relieved to find she had finally settled down. The dull ache was back in his leg. He had been on it too long. Had it not been for following Miss Taffy all afternoon, he would have made camp a long time ago.

He eased overboard into hip-deep water. A light crunch of shell touched his bare feet. He untied his bandaged leg, working it back and forth underwater to increase his circulation, all the time wondering about Miss Taffy. How much did she know about the swamp? She had already come into it a good distance. Could she find her way out again? Did she know how big the swamp really was? And about the gooey black mud fanning out for miles in the back parts? Jody resolved again to keep a close watch over her.

Feeling refreshed, he climbed back into his boat. He poured peroxide into his wound and rinsed the bandage out. Dusk settled over the swamp. He spread a quilt over the seat and stretched out. He would sleep with one eye open, he told himself, and keep a watch. He looked toward the sandbar. Miss Taffy was sleeping peacefully.

≈

Sometime during the night, Jody awakened with a start. For a moment he couldn't remember where he was. He was lying in a cramped position with one leg stretched full length in front of him, the other dangling in the water. His first impression, when he opened his eyes to total darkness, was that something had awakened him. He lay still and listened.

The only sound was the gentle lapping of water at the sides of the boat. Then he remembered. He was anchored on the lee side of a small island in Cranes Bog some hundred or so yards from the sandbar where Miss Taffy had bedded down for the night. He unwound himself from his quilt. The back of his neck hurt from sleeping with his head propped against the boat railing. He rubbed sleep from his eyes and felt a light south wind touch his face. He looked at the sky. A blanket of stars stared back through the deep void. He wondered how long he had been sleeping.

When his eyes became adjusted to the dark, he stood up, at once feeling cold dampness under his feet. He peered through the branches in the direction of the sandbar. There was nothing but darkness.

24

Small lapping sounds under the mangroves told Jody the tide was coming in. He made a quick calculation. Slack tide should have been sometime around midnight.

He swore under his breath. What time was it now? Two o'clock, or even later? How could he have slept like that? Other nights, the soreness in his leg would have brought him awake at odd intervals.

He fumbled in the dark to pull in his anchor, intent on checking things out. He slid the skiff out of the mangroves and shoved off.

If only he could see!

When he felt the bow of his skiff nudging the edge of the sandbar, he eased overboard and carefully set the anchor. He stood still, straining his eyes to pick up the outline of Miss Taffy's boat, but all he could see was the gray-white blur of sand at his feet. Slowly, so as not to trip over anything, he began to walk, expecting at any moment to see Miss Taffy's skiff in front of him. The farther he went without seeing anything, the more concerned he became. Then, to add to his alarm, he found himself back at his own boat!

He scowled, trying to come up with some explanation as to why Miss Taffy would pull up stakes and leave in the dark. It didn't make any sense! The more he thought about it, the more he became convinced that she had not gone off of her own accord. Something had happened. He was sure of it!

He fumbled under his head cap for a flashlight and clicked it on, swinging the small arc of light over the sand. Fiddler crabs scurried out of his way. He retraced his steps, shining the light in all directions, cursing himself for not having made contact with Miss Taffy when he'd had the opportunity. It would have been a simple matter to tell her that he wasn't snooping, that he was leaving home and wasn't particularly interested in anyone knowing his business either. She might even have been glad to see him.

He slowed when he came to the part of the bar where he had seen her boat snubbed up onshore. He played the beam over the sand, looking for the marks made by the bow resting on the bottom. There was nothing. The tide had washed everything away.

Just then something caught his eye. When he centered the beam on an object at his feet, he felt a sudden emptiness in the pit of his stomach. There, half hidden in the dry sand, was a small, steel gray anchor.

Jody stood still, staring at it while the implications of the whole thing came to him. Now he knew. Sometime during the night, while Miss Taffy slept, her bowline had worked loose. At this very moment she might still be asleep, aimlessly drifting about the swamp with the incoming tide. A light wind was blowing from the south. Under these conditions, there was only one way a boat would drift—deeper and deeper into the bowels of the swamp!

Jody broke out in a cold sweat. He had to find Miss Taffy, no matter what. Once she awakened to what was happening, she could be hopelessly lost.

He picked up the anchor and headed back to his boat, trying to figure out the best course of action. Because the tide had been going out when she'd stopped at the sandbar, Jody felt certain she would have been aground there at least until the tide started in. It was probably the action of the incoming tide that had worked her bowline loose. In that case, Miss Taffy might have been drifting for several hours or more.

There was only one thing to do—get in his skiff and go where the tide and wind dictated. At least he would be heading in the same general direction as Miss Taffy. He would call into the night, hoping she would hear him. Beyond that, there was little else he could do until daylight.

He crawled into his skiff and shoved off.

26

≈ 5 ≈

The first pale hint of dawn was just breaking over the swamp when Taffy stirred restlessly on the seat of her skiff. She was feeling the same terrible desolation that she had experienced every morning, upon awakening, since her grandfather's death. All she wanted to do was slip back to sleep and never have to face the pain of her loss again. Dandy was gone from her forever. She couldn't bear it.

The ache in her throat brought her awake. Tears welled up in her eyes. She pulled the quilt tighter about her and wept while she waited for the grief to run its course.

The harshness of the bare seat under her body reminded her of her surroundings. She was in Cranes Bog. She had fallen asleep on the stern seat of her boat. She opened her eyes to a curtain of heavy fog. Visibility was no more than a few feet in any direction. The fog was like a wall around her, sealing her off from the rest of the world. As her eyes adjusted, she became aware of vague outlines taking shape like apparitions in the gloom. Off to one side, the blur of a small mangrove island, seen, yet not seen, dimly came into view, then evaporated before her eyes. She tossed the quilt aside and sat up, sending Tar Baby, who had been sleeping beside her, abruptly to his feet.

She sat still, looking into the dark, oily smooth water, trying to shake off the feeling of disorientation that the eerie surroundings had produced. Then memories of the preceding day flooded in. Snakes in the mangroves. The bone-tired feeling of fatigue. The sand island where she had anchored the skiff.

The sand island!

She scrambled to her feet, straining her eyes for a glimpse of the white shoreline, but could see nothing in the fog. Then she saw the slack angle of the bowline. Part of it was floating in the water, the rest submerged.

She snatched at the rope. It was weightless—nothing fetched up.

The anchor was gone!

She drew in the rest of the line and dropped it in the bottom of the boat. Her mouth felt dry. She shivered. When had she lost the anchor? How far had she drifted? Where was she now?

It wasn't so much the loss of the anchor that troubled Taffy. She could always improvise. The thing that hit her hardest was the fact that she had lost all her bearings. She had no idea how long she had been drifting or where she was now. Head south to find the exits, her grandfather had said. But where was south? She didn't know. She was lost and frightened.

The more she thought about it, the more upset she became. She paced the small confines of the boat. What would her grandfather do if he were here now? Surely there were no landmarks in Cranes Bog to go by. No tall pines on a distant shore. No Indian shell mounds or other traces of civilization. Nothing but the sameness everywhere of water and mangroves.

She didn't know what Dandy would do, but she had a gut feeling her grandfather wouldn't be lost at all. He would know where he was and how to get out. But how? What would he go by to guide him?

Then, suddenly, she knew what her grandfather would rely on. *The tide!* Why hadn't she thought of it before?

There were only two ways the tide could go: north on the incoming, south on the outgoing. It was as simple as that.

She looked down at the water. It was not moving. The tide had reached its peak and was in a resting period before the change. She could tell from the small, undulating ripple on the surface. Once the water started to move, she would know all she needed to know about directions.

Taffy settled down, content to wait for the tide to change, as well as for the brighter light of day. She looked into the pail at her feet where the clams were closed tight. She picked up two of them and, holding one in each hand, banged them together to break the heavy shells. Juice streamed through her fingers. She picked out the broken bits of shell and put the meat in her mouth. Tar Baby moved to join her in the meal.

She was still munching clams when the shifting fog began to lift. The scene around her was unlike any part of the swamp she had seen before. The prop roots showing under the mangroves on nearby islands were not glossy red but dingy brown, with a covering of rotting, hairlike moss. Mud spits lay barren and ugly in the pale light. There were no birds overhead. No herons in the shallows. Except for the green leaves of the mangroves, all color in the swamp was swallowed up in mud, slime, and dinginess. The water was muddy, and she couldn't see bottom. There was a smell of decay in the air. The area was depressing, and she wanted to get away.

When the tide change came, patches of sea grass began to move in the water in a sluggish, outward flow to the south. It was time for Taffy to go. She picked up the poling oar and shoved it to bottom, leaning her weight on it to set the skiff in motion. The boat leaped forward, then fetched up so abruptly that Taffy all but lost her balance. The oar blade was stuck in the bottom, refusing to budge. She yanked and pulled, twisting and turning it in her hands, until at last it broke free. A thick gob of mud clung to it when she brought it up.

She sank the pole again, this time with a slow, cautious prod. The resistance was the same. She pulled the blade free and threw the oar to the bottom of the boat. *She was stranded in a sea of rotting mud!* The poling oar was useless. The tide was too sluggish to be of any use, and there was no wind to help her.

She glared into the silent swamp. How far away were the sand islands? The nesting birds? The pale green water where she had dug clams and seen the small fish darting around?

She had to get out of here, but how? She thought about the paddle she had left behind at the shack. Why hadn't she brought it along? The boat was already too cluttered, she had told herself. There simply wasn't room. Besides, she hadn't expected to get caught in a mess like this.

Taffy knew she could use the poling oar as a paddle, but at best it would be a slow and tiring process. The blade was narrow, the poling oar heavy. She had to come up with something better.

In the end she tied small mangrove branches to both ends of the poling oar and, with slow, steady sweeps through the water, managed to get the skiff moving along at a respectable pace.

≈ 6 ≈

A sudden blast of chill wind whipped out of the north, riling the water into a froth of small whitecaps. Fingers of lightning streaked across the sky, followed by sharp claps of thunder. There was a smell of rain in the air. The storm that had been making up since yesterday was ready to erupt.

As fast as she could, Taffy headed for the nearest mangrove island. She guided the skiff around to the lee side and slipped the bow up under the branches. Once she was behind the island, the main force of the wind died.

She peered into the foliage overhead, then into the tangle of prop roots in the water. She searched the shoreline, then let her breath out slowly. No snakes in sight.

After securing the bowline and spreading the tarpaulin overhead, she sat down to wait out the storm. She could already hear the hiss of pelting rain on the water.

The storm broke overhead with a roar. Wind tore at the tops of the trees, furiously twisting the branches. Rain filtered through the branches like a mist, forming small streams that dribbled off the edges of the tarpaulin. It was no more than eight o'clock in the morning, Taffy calculated, but the gloom was like the fall of night. Tar Baby didn't like it. He lay his ears back at the sound of the wind and eyed the restless water slopping against the sides of the boat. He crawled into Taffy's lap and buried his head in the crook of her arm.

The fresh smell of rain did little to tone down the stench of decay under the mangroves. Rancid gumbo—decaying sea grass—lay matted around the roots. Mud and dead leaves lined the shore. Everything reeked of deterioration. It was beyond Taffy's imagination how any living creature could tolerate such a place, yet life seemed to flourish. Small black crabs walked upside down under the branches. Sea roaches, their bodies almost invisible against the wet bark, scurried about. Drab-colored coon oysters hung in clumps at the end of each ropelike prop root, while horseshoe crabs lumbered about in the edge of the water like nomads from another world.

Taffy shivered. A cold wind touched the back of her neck, and goose bumps appeared on her arms. She reached in the storage compartment and brought out a bright yellow slicker and rain hat that buckled under her chin. She snuggled into it gratefully.

As the day dragged on, her restlessness increased. The thunder and lightning finally subsided, and the north wind dwindled to a crisp breeze. Still, the rain poured down with a vengeance. Small leaks found their way into the tarpaulin, dribbling water over the gear and forming puddles in the bottom of the boat.

She and Tar Baby ate more of the clams. She sopped up water with a sponge. She caught rainwater and refilled the water jugs.

Tar Baby slept on the stern seat, wadded up in a tight ball with his paws covering his face. Moisture glistened on his fur. Taffy looked at him with envy. She pulled the slicker tighter about her and curled up beside him.

Water continued to slap at the sides of the boat. Taffy slept, dreaming the same dream over and over: She was in a cold and colorless world of shadow, mist, and ugliness. She strained to get away, but something held her back. Her feet felt heavy. Just as she lost all hope, she found herself standing on the shore of Little Placid Bay, her grandfather's shack in front of her. The sun was shining. Unspeakable joy overwhelmed her as she raced up the gangplank and pushed open the screen door, feeling the warmth and comfort of familiar surroundings. She was home!

Taffy slowly came awake to the sound of rain on the water. She lay still, the euphoric feeling quickly draining away. She wasn't home—she was stuck in Cranes Bog in a downpour that wouldn't stop. The contrast was devastating. Searing pangs of homesickness poured through her. If only she could race up that gangplank once more! Why had she ever left?

With tears on her cheeks, she groped for Tar Baby at her side, but the place where he had been was empty. She sat up with a start, her eyes darting around the boat. Tar Baby was nowhere in sight. She searched the wet tangle of mangroves onshore, screaming the cat's name over and over, hysterically.

There was no response, only the sound of rain falling through the trees. Already a terrible emptiness was filling the boat, reminding Taffy of her need for the little animal who had shared so much with her.

She listened to her last urgent call fade away. She had to find him, even if it meant crawling around on her hands and knees under the mangroves. She had to have him back!

Slowly, her reasoning returned. The island was small. The cat wouldn't stray far, not with rain splattering down and mud oozing between his toes. He had gone ashore to relieve himself. He would come back. *He had to!*

Dusk was falling. She reached under the canvas covering for the lantern. She lifted the lid to the storage compartment and found matches. The lantern's glow brought a small touch of cheerfulness to the dreary surroundings. Tar Baby would see it. It would hurry him on his way back to her. She set it on the seat and began sopping water out of the bottom of the boat again.

Taffy felt the cat's presence even before she saw him. She glanced up just in time to see him leap to the bow like a black apparition appearing silently in the gathering darkness.

She dropped the sponge, squealing in delight as she scrambled to her feet and gathered him in her arms, unmindful of the mud that dripped down her slicker. Tar Baby's fur was plastered to his body, giving him a rakish, grotesque appearance. She sponged him clean and dried him as best she could, then held him close to her to warm his body. Tar Baby looked as happy to be back on the boat as she was to have him there.

≈

There were six clams left in the pail. Taffy cracked one and ate all the meat except the orange-colored lip, which she kept for fish bait. She dropped the shell overboard. If there were any minnows lurking around in the water, she knew they would be quick to nibble at the bits of meat left in the shell. She reached in her pocket and brought out a fishline with a tiny fishhook on it. She pinched off a small piece of the clam lip, baited the hook, and dropped it over the side of the boat. Within seconds she caught a small black chub. Tar Baby ate it greedily. The meal went on until Taffy had finished the clams and Tar Baby was full of chubs.

She knew now, with darkness closed in around her, just how long the night was going to be. She was stuck under the mangroves until daybreak, whether the rain stopped or not. At best, it wasn't a pleasant prospect, but it was all she had.

She took off her rain hat and worked the rubber band out of her hair. A tangled mass of hair fell around her shoulders. She found a comb and tried to use it, but the combination of salt air, sweat, and lack of care since she had left home was too much. The comb snagged even the smallest strand of hair. She tossed it on the seat and glared into the lantern. Was this how it was going to be from now on? She couldn't even deal with her hair!

She thought about all the days and nights ahead. For a while at least, one would be just like another. Sleeping and eating on the boat. Endless poling. Tomorrow she would find her way back to the sand islands and the clear green waters. She would hang around there until enough time had passed so that she would feel safe to move on. Under the cover of darkness, she would pick up where she had left off. Head for the gulf and follow the coastline. Keep going until she was sure the village was far enough away so that there would be no possibility of her being recognized. She would take her time checking out a suitable place to settle down. A deserted island on the bay side with fresh water, one within poling distance of a fish house. She would put up a tent. Catch fish and take them to market.

That was going to be just fine, Taffy thought, once she was settled down. For now, what was she going to do with her tangled mess of hair?

She rummaged through the storage compartment and brought out a small mirror and a pair of scissors. She sat on the seat with the mirror wedged between her knees. The long hair would have to go.

She picked up the scissors and, with slow deliberation, separated a small strand of hair and snipped it off short. Then another, and another. As she worked, her face became a study in concentration. The tip of her tongue slid from one corner of her mouth to the other. Tar Baby watched with mild interest as the snipping sounds continued and the pile of hair grew higher.

When she finished, she ran her fingers through the soft curls left on her head. She felt strangely light-headed. She looked in the mirror again and smiled at her reflection. The new haircut gave her a kind of chic look. She ran the comb through her hair. No snags, no tangles to fetch up in the teeth. She had done a good job.

It was while she was putting her things back in the storage compartment that a painful thought came to mind and stuck there. Her smile vanished. If her grandfather could see her now, it would break his heart!

She could see him looking at her shorn head, disappointment on his face. She stared blindly into the dark mangroves beyond the circle of light, feeling a tightness in her throat. She could almost hear his proud voice, see the ice blue eyes kindle with pleasure when she would undo the rubber bands and brush her long waves into place. "Your crowning glory, lass," he had said so often. "Like fine gold and platinum spun together."

She stared mutely at the pile of hair at her feet. A sob came to her throat. She got up quickly and pitched the hair overboard. For a moment it lay in a wad on top of the water, then, slowly, the long tresses began to break apart.

Her mouth felt dry. She snatched up the rain hat and jammed it back on her head. She flounced down on the seat, shoved her chin in her hands, and glared into the mangroves again.

≈

The night wore on, bringing little change. There was no letup in the rain. Taffy had to move the lantern away from overhead leaks to keep it dry. She spent a good deal of time sopping up water.

All during that time, thoughts of her grandfather weighed heavy on her mind. It wasn't only her haircut that bothered her. What would he think of her closing up the shack and taking off in his skiff to hide in the wilds until the welfare authorities no longer had any interest in her? What would he think of her now, lost in the mud flats in Cranes Bog?

Loneliness dogged her. She was sick and tired of the incessant rain. Then, just when she felt most despondent, a strange and indescribable glow of wonderment passed through her. *She could actually feel her grandfather's presence!*

She sat very still, arms tight to her body, eyes closed. It was as though he were right in the boat with her. The impression of his nearness was real enough to bring tears to her eyes. And yet, there was no feeling of sadness connected with the impression, only a deep sense of wonderment. The feeling passed.

Taffy sat for a long time thinking about what had just happened. She wasn't certain, of course. But she *was* certain of one thing: Her grandfather, wherever he was, had somehow come to her. For a short time he had been right on the boat with her. She had felt his love surging through her, filling her with a strange and wonderful sense of peace.

≈

No longer irritated by the water that continued to dribble into the boat, Taffy let her thoughts drift from one memory of her grandfather to another. The one that came to her most often was the evening when she had met him for the first time.

She was four years old when the news came to her from Mrs. Stenstrom, the social worker in Boston. Taffy lived there with foster parents. The authorities, Mrs.

Stenstrom said, had managed to track down her grandfather, who lived in a fishing village on the west coast of
Florida. Arrangements were being made for her to make
the trip south to live with him.

At first, Taffy had felt excited. A real live grandfather
of her own! But when she said good-bye to Mrs. Stenstrom at the depot and boarded the train, thoughts of the
unknown ahead frightened her. What would her grandfather be like? Would he be old and grumpy, maybe
wishing she hadn't come to live with him? She wished
her mother was alive. She missed Mrs. Stenstrom, who
sometimes took her home with her on weekends.

Hour after hour, as the train sped past the frozen
landscape, Taffy thought about her instructions from
Mrs. Stenstrom. Smile brightly to show her grandfather
that she was happy to be with him. Do not address him
as "sir" or "mister": Call him "Grandfather." First im-
pressions were important, Mrs. Stenstrom had said. More
than anything else, Taffy wanted to please her grandfather because she did not want to be sent off to another
foster home.

It was dusk when the conductor gently nudged her
awake. The train had finally brought her to her destination. She bundled up the coat and sweater she had shed
along the way and stepped out into the warm night air.
A chill passed through her as fear closed in.

"Taffy . . ."

Someone called her name. She stood still, listening. It
was a nice voice—warm, gentle, friendly. It made her feel
good inside. At first, all she was able to see was a tall,
massive frame towering above others milling around, and
the short-cropped, curly white hair on his head. Then
the ice blue eyes smiled at her, a flash of strong white
teeth in the leather-skinned face. It was the nicest face
she had ever seen.

To be sure, Taffy gave him her best smile. But when

she tried to say "Grandfather," the stammerings that had so often plagued her speech poured out in a rush, and in a very small voice all she managed was "Gran . . . Gran . . . dandy. . . ."

He knelt down, gathering her in his big arms, murmuring over and over, "Taffy . . . My little Taffy. . . ." She could still remember the clean scent of salt air about him, the roughness of his cheek on hers, but she never understood the reason for her flood of tears that followed. He held her tightly in his arms, saying nothing, while she wept on his shoulder. When she looked up, he was still smiling at her. There was moisture in his eyes. She dried her tears, knowing in that moment she could love this new grandfather of hers with all her heart.

And that was the way it had been, Taffy reflected. She had loved him from the beginning, and over the years her love had grown deeper. At no time in her life had she envied other children for their parents. With Dandy, there had been no need. He had been father, mother, friend, and companion, all in one.

Under the mangroves, Taffy had become so lost in her thoughts of her grandfather that she didn't notice the lantern burning low until the flame flickered, then died. The shock of finding herself in total darkness gave new life to Taffy's senses. Something was different about the sounds of the swamp around her. She closed her eyes and listened, then looked up quickly. The incessant roar of the downpour was missing. All she could hear now were the soft patterings of a light drizzle.

She stood up. Her eyes had begun to adjust. She looked about. Mangrove branches were beginning to take on shape. She could see vague outlines of gnarled prop roots standing in the water. Overhead, dim light filtered through.

Daylight was coming!

She turned to look out through the small open space where the curtain of rain had held her prisoner for so long. A soft, silvery mist played over the surface of the water. The storm clouds had lifted. A faint glow showed in the east. It was time to move on!

≈ 7 ≈

Taffy came out of the mangroves, enchanted. The silvery mists of predawn had filtered over the swamp, transforming it into a mystical world. A single star twinkled overhead. Mangrove leaves glistened, washed clean of dust and salt crystals.

The skiff drifted about lazily on the calm water while Taffy tied more branches to the poling oar. With rising spirits, she set the boat in motion. Tar Baby took up his position on the head cap.

Once in open water, Taffy was quick to note the light north breeze. Within minutes, she put up a makeshift sail, using a shirt attached to a gig handle. The sail hung limp for a moment, then caught, billowing out to full capacity. She was on her way.

Time passed quickly. The sun came up, steaming dampness from the boat. From time to time, she tested the bottom, but it was still too muddy to pole. Where were the birds? The sand islands? How much farther would she have to go to get out of this place?

Around noon, the breeze died. The shirt flapped listlessly, then collapsed. She dismantled her sail and noticed small patches of sea grass floating back into the swamp. The tide was against her.

Tar Baby sat up suddenly. He tensed, sniffing the air, staring over the water. Taffy looked at him. What scent had come to his nose? Or had his keen ears picked up some sound she couldn't detect? His fur bristled as his nose worked. He stood immobile, eyes fixed on the water straight ahead.

Taffy lay the poling oar down and eased toward the bow, straining her eyes over the water. The sun overhead shone brightly, turning the face of the water into a sea of sparkling diamonds. Then something floating on the water caught her eye. A bunched-up wad of sea grass? A piece of driftwood? She shaded her eyes, watching as the object drifted closer. A moment later, a low growl sounded deep in Tar Baby's throat. In a burst of recognition, she saw the object take on shape, color, and form. The thing floating on the water was a large, evil-looking rattlesnake!

Tar Baby, in an awkward, half-crouched position, appeared to have turned to stone. Taffy stood mesmerized, staring in horror at the narrow black tongue sliding in and out of the snake's mouth while the reptile floated about three yards off the bow.

Her mind raced. There was no time to move the boat— the rattler was already too close. All she could do now was pray that the reptile would just keep on drifting. Please, God, don't let it uncoil and swim for the boat!

Without taking her eyes off the snake, she slowly eased her hand in back of her to close her fingers around the poling oar. The snake saw her movement and gave warning with the whirring vibrations of its rattle on the end of its tail.

It was a moment Taffy would never forget: The deadly fangs only a few feet away; the pungent, musky odor like sour cucumbers filling the air; the terrible closeness.

With her hand still gripping the pole, Taffy watched, not daring to draw a breath. Moments ticked on. Tar Baby, still holding his position on the bow, stared at the snake in fixed concentration as the reptile slowly drifted, inch by inch, foot by foot, until at last it cleared the stern of the boat and floated on.

Taffy slumped down on the head cap, her face the color of ashes.

"You were telling me as plain as you could, Tar. I should have known. . . ."

By now the rattler was nothing more than a small dot on the water. Where had it come from? Where was it going? Why was it here at all? Rattlesnakes were dry-land critters, Dandy had told her. They didn't like water much.

Then she remembered something else her grandfather had told her. *Big rattlers traveled in pairs.* She bounded to her feet, scanning the waters again in all directions. Another big rattler could be floating right behind the one she had just seen. She would not be caught unawares a second time.

When she was satisfied that there were no more snakes in sight, Taffy picked up the cat and held him tight.

"I'm depending on you Tar. Keep that nose working." With that, she slipped back to the stern area and picked up the oar.

As she paddled on, Taffy recalled other things her grandfather had told her about rattlers. When a water source dried up, or food was hard to come by, rattlers moved from one place to another by coiling up on top of the water and letting the tide or wind carry them. Yet they were not at ease on the water, he had said. Always looking for a floating object to crawl up on. A log. A piece of driftwood. A boat.

Taffy shuddered. What if that big reptile had chosen her boat to crawl into?

She paddled on. The pace was slow, and her back ached. Blisters formed on her hands, which itched to pole the skiff the way it was supposed to be poled. Just as she was beginning to relax, she saw Tar Baby's body stiffen again. He was staring this time to the starboard side.

She frantically searched the water, dreading what she might find. Still holding the poling oar, she made her way forward. There, in the distance, she saw them floating high on the water. Not the heavy bulk of a big rattler, but two smaller ones, neatly coiled, side by side. As she watched them drift, a sense of impending evil began to take form in her mind, an instinct born of a sixth sense. Something ugly was shaping up in the swamp.

Seeing a rattler on the water wasn't common, yet three had floated by within a matter of minutes. . . .

Dry-land creatures, Dandy had said. She gripped the pole tight in her hand as horror flashed through her. *The rattlesnakes in Cranes Bog had been flooded out with all that rain! They had taken to the water in search of higher ground. They were out there on the water now, in countless numbers, coming her way. . . .*

"This ghastly place," she hissed through clenched teeth. "This miserable, godforsaken place!"

Then Tar Baby relaxed. He was panting, so Taffy filled his water pan and set it down beside him. She reached under the bow and brought out the three-pronged gig she had used to mount the sail. She tested the prongs.

A poling oar, a gig, two pairs of eyes, and a cat's nose for warning signals. It wasn't the best defense against a charge of rattlers, but it was all she had. She put the gig in a handy place, picked up the poling oar, and moved on.

A dry sandbar. That was what she needed. A place on firm ground to ward off the rattlers. She scowled into the distance. A mud spit loomed nearby, ugly and barren. Not a likely place to find firm ground, but she would check it out.

As the boat moved toward the spit, Taffy thought of other possibilities. What would the rattlers do once the tide turned? Would they have sense enough to take refuge in the mangrove islands, waiting for the next tide to take them closer to the mainland? Or would they simply float back again the way they had come?

She chewed on her lip, wondering how Dandy would reason that out. She remembered him telling her there was a big difference between the behavior of large rattlers and smaller ones. The large ones, he had said, had plenty of sense. Kept to themselves in the deep woods, seldom venturing out. They were cautious, but when a person came close, the big rattlers never backed off. They stood their ground, letting their presence be known with a warning rattle.

Not so with the smaller rattlers, Dandy had cautioned. They were ill-tempered, feisty, and unpredictable. Because their rattles were few and undeveloped, they lacked self-assurance. Often as not, they would strike first and warn later.

That, of course, spelled out a lot of the rattlers' behavior on dry land, but it told Taffy very little of what to expect from them on the water at the turn of the tide. She doubted even her grandfather could predict that. Chances were, if he were here to venture a guess, he would say the big ones would probably know enough to wind themselves around the mangrove branches and wait out the tide. What the smaller ones might do would be anybody's guess.

Taffy wasn't certain about anything except that the rattlers had probably been flooded out. After all, it had rained for almost seventeen hours. It could be days, maybe weeks before the swamp got back to normal. In the meantime . . .

The slant of the sun on the water told Taffy it must be close to two o'clock. In time, night would fall, turning Cranes Bog into a place of watery blackness with countless numbers of rattlers floating around.

Just then, the bow of the skiff touched the mud spit. Slate-colored pieces of shell lay half buried in the bleak surface. She looked at it, unseeing.

What was she doing here? Why had she thought she might take refuge on this place? She had to get out of the swamp—now!

Tar Baby growled, and Taffy whipped around. The cat was staring at the mud island, fur bristling. A big rattler came into view as it wound a trail over the surface of the spit. Taffy watched, sucking in her breath and tightening her grip on the poling oar. The snake became aware of her, and, within seconds, it coiled.

She shoved the boat back into open water. By now, her fear had become a part of her. Common sense told her that every rattler within range of that mud spit would stop, just as that one had done. And it would be the same on a dry sandbar.

She paddled on furiously, heading the boat in a southerly direction. *She had to find her way out of the swamp before dusk.* She would take advantage of every minute left in the day. There would be no more inspections. No rest periods. No stops for anything!

In her mind, she could see the darkness creeping over the water, the dim outline of the islands slipping by in the gloom. She could feel the eerie stillness settling over the bog as dusk congealed into night. She would light the lantern, but the small flame would offer little consolation. Then would come the terrible waiting. . . .

At that moment, she saw the cat lift his head, sniff the air, then rise to his feet. Seeing nothing on the water, she glanced at the cat again. His fur lay smooth, yet his nose worked constantly.

Taffy stopped paddling. Moments ticked by. A light breeze brought a faint, unfamiliar scent to her nostrils, then the fragile odor was gone. She felt sure that the scent did not belong in the swamp. It wasn't dead sea

46

grass, salt air, mangrove blossoms, decayed roots, or dried mud. Whatever it was that she had smelled, it had nothing to do with these things.

She breathed deeply in an attempt to pick it up again, and there it was, strong, pungent, and unmistakable.

Smoke! She was sure of it! But how could that be? Back in the bowels of a rained-out swamp? There couldn't possibly be a dry stick of wood in the entire bog, so how could something be burning? It didn't make sense.

She stared into the distance. Nothing stirred except the small patches of sea grass moving slowly by the boat. Then she saw it. In the distance, behind a small green island, a dense column of smoke rose serenely in the air. She gaped, openmouthed as she watched it climb higher. Stray wisps broke away and vanished. Within seconds, more smoke billowed out over the tops of the trees and spread over the water.

Another human being was in the swamp! Right on the other side of that island!

Excitement brought a flush to Taffy's cheeks. That fire! Whoever had built it was caught in the same situation as she, and was using the smoke to ward off the rattlers. Somehow, that person had been fortunate enough to find a strip of firm ground in this grizzly, oozing part of the bog.

Taffy hastily set her skiff in motion, wondering about the person. Had he, too, come into the swamp and lost his way? What kind of person would she find? An old hermit—the kind of person dogs followed around? Or would she find someone who was afraid of people, wild and strange? If he wasn't a loner living in the wilds, maybe he was someone hiding from the law. A bootlegger? A thief? A murderer?

Taffy slackened her pace. Some of her enthusiasm left her. She chewed at her lip. The boat dawdled while she tried to put her thoughts into perspective. After all, she told herself, there was no reason to believe the stranger was a fugitive simply because he was in the swamp. And she wasn't going to worry about some old hermit, either. Besides, who in their right mind would expect to find a *girl* wandering around in this muddy, snake-infested place?

She ran her fingers through her short crop of hair. She looked down at her baggy khakis rolled up to her knees, her grimy bare feet. Her body was lean, hard, and tanned. There were no bulges in the wrong places. She could easily pass for a boy.

She picked up the straw hat. Frayed ends stuck out in all directions. She jammed it on her head, tilting it at a rakish angle. She spit over the side of the boat and, picking up the poling oar, set her course for the island.

≈ 8 ≈

The skiff slowly came to a stop as the bow nudged into branches at the tip of the island. Taffy peered cautiously through the leaves, spreading the branches and craning her neck for a better look. Stretching out in a span of a hundred yards or so was the green shoreline, the clear view ending abruptly in clouds of white smoke. The clouds spilled over the water, obscuring everything but the stern of a small skiff lying at anchor in the calm water. As she watched, the smoke began to break up and trail away. Through it she saw the orange-red glow of a fire, and, as the moments went by and more air cleared, she was able to see something else, something that brought new excitement.

There, like an oasis in the desert, was a well-established sandbar rising out of the water in a clear, graceful arc. This was not just another of the mud spits she had been seeing all morning. It was gray-white, indicating a combination of fine shell and sand. The remains of an age-old Indian shell mound perhaps, or countless layers of broken pieces of shell, stockpiled by busy currents in that one isolated place.

She stared at it, unable to take her eyes away. One clean shell spit in an endless sea of rotting mud! She couldn't believe it!

She longed to leave the cramped quarters of her boat

and walk around on the bar's clean surface. But first she wanted to get a look at the person occupying it.

By now, the smoke was rising in a straight column, affording a clear view of the area.

There was no one in sight.

Off to one side of the fire she saw a small woodpile made up of green mangroves and odd-sized pieces of driftwood. Nearby lay sea grass. Piled up on the shore was a layout of gear: two canvas bags, a coil of rope, a water pail, and, leaning against the mangroves, a poling oar, a paddle, and a cane fishing pole.

Taffy's eyes strayed back to the skiff. It was long and slender, designed for net fishing like her own. Its weathered sides, void of paint, were the same color as the dark water. She might have been looking at her own boat.

No hermit living in the wilds, Taffy reasoned. This person was not established enough for that. Whoever it was had only recently come to this place. He apparently had had little time for anything other than to chop wood to keep his fire going. More than likely, she reasoned further, he was traveling alone. His skiff, along with the gear he was carrying, would be comfortable enough for one person. Two would overcrowd it.

Just then, a figure emerged from the mangroves carrying an armload of green wood. He was small, bent and stooped like an old man. A straw hat covered his head. He stood in the clearing, wiping sweat from his face.

She watched the figure move slowly over to the woodpile, his step awkward, unsteady, open shirt flapping at his sides. His pants legs were rolled up to his knees, exposing a pair of darkly tanned, bony legs.

Taffy let her breath out slowly. A harmless, crippled old man. Her first impulse was to help him, to relieve him of the heavy load he was carrying and seat him in a comfortable place in the shade. She would take up his hatchet and chop wood herself while he rested.

She saw the man stop at the woodpile, the dark red-colored wood spill to the ground. The figure limped to the fire, knelt down, and began pitching the charred ends of burning wood back into the flame.

As she watched, a subtle perception way back in her mind began to surface. There was something vaguely familiar about this figure, something she couldn't put her finger on. Was it the way he carried himself that reminded her of someone?

The person slowly rose from his kneeling position. He turned, looking out over the waters in all directions as though in search of something. He took off his hat and brushed a shock of dark hair out of his eyes.

Taffy stared openmouthed! The person had the face of Jody Hillard!

No, she told herself. It couldn't possibly be Jody. It was only someone who looked like him from a distance. Jody wouldn't be here in Cranes Bog. Taffy had seen him only a few days ago hobbling in the graveyard in Bayview. He would have more sense than to come to this place. He would have no reason.

But she was looking right at him, and there was no mistake. It *was* Jody. She felt like laughing and crying at the same time as she nudged the boat out of the mangroves and picked up the poling oar. *Jody Hillard! The scrubby little rag-mop from the village!* She was never so glad to see anybody in her life.

Jody was still searching the water when Taffy's skiff came into view around the tip of the island. She saw him catch sight of her. He quickly jerked his hat off and waved it in the air, shouting her name over and over. "Miss Taffy! Miss Taffy!"

Jody was obviously beside himself and paced back and forth at the edge of the bar.

The boat slowed to a stop at the edge of shore. Tar Baby leaped to firm ground. For a brief moment neither

Taffy nor Jody spoke. They just stared at each other. Then, all at once, a flood of words tumbled from Taffy's mouth. "Jody! I couldn't believe it when I saw you. How come you're here in Cranes Bog? How did you find this place? How long you been in the swamp? How did you ever get that fire going? Oh, Jody, am I ever glad to see you!"

Jody looked at her, grinning from ear to ear. He reached out to snub the bow of her skiff closer to shore. "Seems like we both got ourselves in a mess of trouble coming to this place, Miss, but since we did, I'm glad you saw my smoke and came here."

Jody could feel the flush creeping into his face. For some reason he felt awkward, tongue-tied. He fidgeted with the buttons on his shirt. He was the little boy again, watching the pretty girl from behind a stack of fish boxes on Mr. Tanner's docks.

Then the feeling passed. Piece by piece, the threads of his own worth came back. After all, things were different now. He was in a position to offer this girl the safety of his hard-earned fire. All his frenzied hours of toil and sweat had paid off. Miss Taffy had joined him, greeted him like a long lost friend.

He straightened up and held out his hand to help her ashore.

"Jody," she asked in a quiet voice, "those rattlers floatin' round out there on the water, they don't like smoke, do they?"

"No, Miss," Jody answered easily. "Snakes don't mess around no place where there's any smell of smoke."

Taffy felt her body sag under her own weight. Finding Jody and the fire had brought the relief she so sorely needed, and her muscles all at once were reduced to the consistency of jelly. She took Jody's hand and stepped ashore, feeling her knees buckle under her. She was close to tears.

Without thinking, Jody reached under the bow for her anchor but, of course, came up with nothing but a piece of rope frayed at the end.

"I lost it," Taffy said simply.

Yes, Jody thought. He wondered what she would think now if she knew it was stored under the bow of his boat. He grinned. "I'll take care of it, Miss. I got a spare."

He got the anchor out of his boat and, with deft fingers, began tying her bowline to it. Taffy watched him. Lines of fatigue showed in his face. In fact, she thought, he looked downright haggard. Except for the grin, all other energies seemed to have left him. She ventured a question. "Why are you here, Jody? In the swamp, I mean?"

He stopped his work for the moment to look at her. The grin faded. "I left home, Miss Taffy. This time I won't be going back."

Taffy stared at him, shocked. Something inside her told her to get up and start doing the things that needed doing. Unload her gear. Scrounge up something to eat. Chop wood. Especially chop wood. Still, she couldn't stop herself from prying. "Why, Jody? What happened?"

Her soft voice, almost a whisper, brought a sting of unexpected tears to Jody's eyes. He turned away, busying himself with the rope. He wanted to let the subject drop, but he knew that, sooner or later, he'd have to talk about it. He figured he may as well get it over with.

"Nothing much happened, I guess," he said, his eyes still fixed on the rope. "Figgered I'd be better off on my own." He let his breath out slowly. "You know about my Uncle John, Miss. Won't know I've gone anywhere for a week or so. Won't be very concerned about it when he does find out, either."

Jody's voice was breaking up, and Taffy didn't ask any more questions. A silence fell between them. He glanced at her out of the corner of his eye. She was staring over the water, apparently in deep thought. He asked a question of his own. "Come to think of it, Miss Taffy, strikes me as Cranes Bog is kind of an out-of-the-way place for you, too. Figgered you'd be back in the village with Mr. Tanner and that preacher, gettin' things straightened out after all that happened."

Jody was sorry his words had come out the way they had. He hadn't meant to sound callous, but Miss Taffy didn't seem to notice. She looked up at him. "I left home, too, Jody. I didn't want to, but I had no choice. Old Miss Bessie was breathin' down my neck. She was all set to put me in a foster home. I was supposed to leave with her yesterday morning."

Jody stood in stunned silence. Old Miss Bessie, the welfare agent! He had forgotten all about her!

"I took off in my skiff right after the service Sunday," she went on to say. "Stayed out of sight on the other side of Palm Key so nobody would see me. Figured Miss Bessie would report me missing right off, so I came here to lay low for a while."

Taffy went on to talk about the things that had happened to her since she came into the swamp. The water snakes in the mangroves, the deep mud she had found herself in after drifting all night. "I was lost and scared, Jody. I couldn't pole the skiff."

Jody listened quietly. He saw a pink flush spread into her face when she talked about the rattlers on the water.

". . . the biggest one I ever saw . . . lookin' right at me and buzzin' like crazy . . . then more and more showing up . . . it was like waking up . . . in hell!"

Jody sank down beside her. Miss Taffy was like a bruised and frightened little child. He wanted to put his arms around her and comfort her, but of course he did not. He didn't know what to do. Somehow, he found his voice. "Miss Taffy," he said gently, "I had kind of a messy time with them rattlers myself till I got my fire going this morning. But once it got going good and I got it covered over with sea grass to make some smoke, I ain't seen one since. They're out there, and will be for a spell till the swamp dries up some, but they won't be showin' up nowhere round this island."

Taffy looked at him steadily, hanging on to every word.

"We got nothin' to worry about, Miss. This island is covered in mangroves. All we got to do is chop them." A smile played at his lips. "Besides, you ain't lost now. I know where we are and how to get out of here when the time comes."

Taffy smiled and got to her feet, offering Jody a hand. She picked up the hatchet where Jody had dropped it. "I'll chop some wood."

Jody was eager to make things as comfortable for Miss Taffy as he could. He finished tying the rope and secured the anchor in the gravel, burying the flanges deep. He unloaded her skiff, putting her clothes and food on high ground, her boat gear next to his own. He scooped up sea grass as it washed ashore, stacking it in mounds beside the fire, all the while keeping an eye on the pot of gruel simmering over a small bed of coals.

While he worked, his thoughts were on Miss Taffy and the pleasure he was feeling at having her safe on the bar with him. Ever since he had crawled out from under his tarpaulin at dawn and seen what was happening with the rattlesnakes, he had been frantic with worry about her. Having her here now seemed like a miracle.

He gathered more sea grass, wishing the ache in his leg would ease up until the work was finished for the night. His whole body was screaming at him to slow up, to stretch out on his back in the sunshine and rest his miserable bones, but that was not possible. Not yet. He scooped up more sea grass.

The afternoon wore on. Shadows lengthened over the swamp, cooling the air as the sun hovered close to the tops of the mangroves. While Taffy chopped wood, she thought about being safe on the bar with Jody, safe from the dark terrors of the night. There was comfort in the thought of a bright fire to burn away the darkness of night, and human company in a desolate swamp. These thoughts goaded her on in her work despite the blisters on her hands.

She thought about Jody. Whatever had happened must have really stirred him up for him to leave home. At least his home had provided a roof over his head. She remembered the times back home when Jody had left the village, not coming back for weeks. No one knew where he went or what he did while he was gone. Everyone took it for granted he would come back when he was ready, and, of course, he always had.

Taffy looked at the waist-high stack of wood. She was pleased with herself. She had done a good job.

Just then, she got a tantalizing whiff of food, setting her appetite aflame. She had never been so hungry!

Jody appeared at her side, his eyes bright with pleasure at the sight of the woodpile. "Gosh, Miss Taffy! Wasn't spectin' all this. You got enough here to last all night."

"You sure, Jody?"

"Yes, Miss. I'm sure."

With that, Taffy stuffed the hatchet handle into the waistband of her pants and gathered up an armload of wood. Jody loaded his own arms.

"Besides, supper is ready."

The thought of food, prepared and ready to eat, brought a smile to Taffy's face. She dumped the wood at the campsite and sank to the ground, grateful for the rest while Jody busied himself around the steaming pot. She threw her hat aside, running her fingers through her hair, and looked at Jody.

Just below the rolled-up pants, she could see a dingy rag around his leg. A dark red stain had seeped through, and angry red flesh showed at the edge of the bandage.

She got up, alarmed, and walked over to him. "What's the matter with your leg, Jody?" she asked.

Jody gave the pot another stir. He glanced up, ready to tell her about his injury, but stopped short, staring at her hair. "Cripes, Miss Taffy," he croaked. "What happened . . . what happened to all your beautiful hair?"

Taffy turned away abruptly. She had forgotten all about her hair. She ran her fingers through it again. In frustration, she turned back to him. There was an edge to her voice. "Nothing *happened*. I cut it off. It was always in the way. It's not important. After all, it *will* grow back."

Jody lowered his eyes. "Didn't mean to offend you, Miss. Guess I just . . ." He didn't finish.

Taffy's tone softened. "It's all right, Jody. Like I said, camping out and long hair don't mix. I found that out. Tell me, do I look funny?"

"Oh, no." Jody brightened. "You look just fine. It's just that you, well, you look different, I guess."

Taffy brought the subject back to Jody. "Your leg, Jody. What's wrong with it?"

"I got tangled up with a catfish fin."

Taffy sucked in her breath. Catfish fin! Getting gouged by one was something fishermen always had to watch out for, like stepping on a stingaree. Part of the fin could break off. Infection could set in. She looked at him thoughtfully. "What are you doing about it?"

Jody told her about the doctor in Bayview, the hot water soakings he needed every day, and the medicine he was carrying with him.

"When was the last time you soaked your leg?"

"Two days, maybe three. Can't remember exactly."

Taffy looked at him. "What are you waiting for, Jody? If you was supposed to soak your leg, why haven't you been doing it?"

"Cripes," he countered, rising to his own defense. "What chance did I have with rain pourin' down all that time? Then, when it did stop, I had a devil of a time starting this fire."

Taffy blushed. Of course he had had no time with all this mess going on. Rattlers crawling around on his bar and sopping wet wood to work with. What was she thinking of?

"Tell you what, Jody. I'll go get a pail of water and set it over the coals so it can be heating while we're eating supper."

Jody looked at her gratefully. "I'll have your grub dished up by the time you get back."

Taffy hurried with her task, wondering what Jody's "grub" consisted of. She was so hungry, she didn't much care as long as it filled her up. She set the pail of water over the coals and sat down next to him. He handed her a full, steaming cup.

Tar Baby, who had spent the afternoon either following Jody as he did his chores or wrapping himself around Taffy's legs while she chopped wood, danced about the pot in anticipation. Jody scooped up a panful for him, blowing at the steam.

"Smells good," Taffy said, digging her spoon deep. "What is it?"

"Fish stew," he answered.

"Where did you get fish?"

"Gigged me a couple of good-sized stingarees this morning while I was scrounging up driftwood. Guess most folks wouldn't mess with eatin' stingarees, but I've had 'em lots of times when I been campin' out. They're real easy to catch."

Taffy had nothing against eating stingaree meat. After all, most any fish—except a slimy old catfish maybe— was edible if you were hungry enough. What she saw in her cup was thick, hot, and full of chunks of white fish meat with potatoes, onions, and something orange-colored that looked like pieces of carrot. A pleased look spread over her face when she tasted it.

She had expected Jody to cook up something simple, like grits with a piece of salt pork, or maybe some rice and beans, but this was no simple concoction. Jody's fish stew was really something! She could even taste some kind of herb in it. "This is super, Jody. I wasn't expecting anything like this out here in the middle of a swamp. Where did you learn to cook like this?"

Jody's eyes glistened with pride. "Miss Daisy taught me, mostly. A long time ago. It was either a case of learning to cook or going hungry. I sorta picked up things as I went along."

Steam was rising from Jody's water pail by the time the meal was over. Taffy rinsed the dishes at the edge of the water and put the pot of stew away. She turned to Jody. "I'll fetch your medicine and fresh bandages."

She rummaged through Jody's gear until she found the little cloth bag he told her about. From the bag, she brought out a bottle of peroxide and a medicine vial with a skull and crossbones on the label. She picked it up gingerly. Through the glass she could see a dark, granulated substance.

Permanganate soakings were not new to Taffy. The only thing was, she had never handled the poison herself. Dandy had always done it for her. The hideous-looking skull on the label gave her the creeps.

At the bottom of the bag she found a roll of bandage. She gathered up her collection and went back to Jody. He had rolled his pants leg above his knee and was slowly unwinding the soiled bandage. He lifted the folds carefully until all the dressing fell away, leaving the raw, open wound exposed. Taffy stared, aghast, at the pus oozing from the ugly, gaping hole. She ran her tongue over her lips, unable to look away. She felt Jody's eyes on her.

"Be different lookin' when I get it cleaned up."

He poured peroxide in the wound. Yellow froth spilled down his leg. He picked up the vial of permanganate and shook crystals into the pail until the water turned purple. He recapped the vial and eased his leg in carefully.

Taffy stared at the ground, unable to speak. Her mouth felt dry, and a cold fear crawled up her back. *Jody's leg was in very bad shape. He might even die out here in this swamp!*

Seeing the distress on her face, Jody spoke. "This stuff works good, Miss Taffy, when I use it right. When I get through here, the red places won't look so red. The hole will be all cleaned out, and, as long as I soak my leg like I'm supposed to, it will stay that way."

Taffy looked at him. He was like a wasted little waif, stretched out on the ground with his knobby knee sticking up over the pail. His shirt was open, exposing sharp ribs under the thin covering of skin. Perspiration glistened on his body. She got out the bedrolls and shook out Jody's quilt, smoothing part of it under his body, the rest under his head for a pillow. She sat down beside him.

"Jody, right now would be a good time to start getting you back in shape. You pulled me out of an awful scrape today. Now it's my turn to do something. From now on, I'll look after things. Cook the meals, chop the wood, and scrounge up sea grass. Maybe even gig some more stingarees. I'll heat your water and wash your bandages. All you have to do is soak your leg and rest up. I'm going to take care of you. Put some color back in your cheeks, and meat on your bones."

The warm, soothing tone of Miss Taffy's voice brought tears to Jody's eyes. Something in her voice brought back vague memories of the warmth and comfort of his mother's arms when he had been a very small boy. No one had made him feel that way since death took his mother away. He blinked the tears back, feeling his body melt into the folds of the quilt. He turned his head to look at her. Flames from the fire cast a soft light on her face. Tears filled his eyes again, and he turned away.

Taffy tossed more wood on the fire. She covered the flames with sea grass and stood back to watch the smoke billow out. She put Jody's water back on the coals to reheat, carefully covering his leg with a fold of the quilt. She brought out ladyfinger bananas from her food stock and spread them beside him. She was tired, yet a restlessness had taken possession of her. She paced back and forth in front of the fire, waiting for the water to heat.

"Where are you headed when your leg gets well enough to travel, Jody?"

Her question brought Jody out of his reverie. "No place, I guess. Least not for a while. Just figured to find me an island some place with fresh water on it and live off the water till something better turns up."

"Do you know about any islands with fresh water?"

Jody took his time answering. "Well yeah, Miss Taffy. Course there's never any on the small islands. None here in the swamp, either. But some of the big islands outside have water. Only thing is, when a dry spell comes along, a lot of 'em dry up. Somebody campin' out needs fresh water the year around. Like that artesian well on Sands Key."

Taffy continued to pace, thinking that Jody's plans weren't much different from her own, except *he* didn't have to hide out from the authorities. He was free to go where he pleased. The villagers were accustomed to his comings and goings. Like he said, no one would miss him.

"Where is Sands Key?"

"About two miles north on the gulf coast after you leave the mouth of Big Placid Bay."

Not far from that little settlement called Hawks Landing, she thought. Sands Key was too close for hiding out.

Jody was aware of the interest he had stirred in Miss Taffy. She had left home to get away from Miss Bessie, had come into the swamp to lay low for a while, but she had said nothing about her future plans. Surely she wasn't figuring on staying here indefinitely. Not wanting to lose the magic of the moment, he spoke. "I know about another island that has fresh water all the time. Long ways from here, though."

"Where?"

"Place called Pelican Island. Sets out in the gulf about a mile or two from the mainland. Has an old abandoned house on the north end and a pitcher pump that works when you prime it."

"Tell me about it," Taffy said, continuing to pace.

"Sets out there in clear blue water with deserted islands on each side and wide passes in between. There's grass flats on the lee side. The old house is made of pecky cypress. Been standing there a long time. There's fruit trees out back. Bananas, mangoes, and coconuts. And that's where the pump is—alongside the house. Don't nobody live round there for miles in any direction."

"How far is it from here?"

"About a hundred miles north after you get out of Big Placid Bay."

Taffy stopped pacing.

"A hundred miles?" she gasped. "You've been that far from home? In your skiff?"

"Yes, Miss," Jody said simply. "I been there several times."

Taffy was speechless. *A hundred miles from Miss Bessie!*

Until now, Jody had had no idea where he would go. Like he said, mess around until something better came along. But now all that was changing. A seed had been planted. It was obvious he had proposed a way out for Miss Taffy, a venture that would take her a long way from the authorities, a place where she would be safe. At the same time, Pelican Island had brought about a very intriguing prospect for himself. He would be in Miss Taffy's company, watch over her, protect her. He would enjoy meals with her. They would do things together. He would never be lonely again!

Taffy found her voice. "Tell me more, Jody. Tell me more about Pelican Island."

≈ 9 ≈

Reverend Hammond, pastor of the Buttonwood Harbor Community Church, stepped off his porch and looked into the heavy mists enveloping the sleeping village around him. Buttoning up his raincoat, he set out down the shell road toward the Tyler bungalow. Even at this early hour, the preacher felt sure the lamps in Miss Bessie's home would be burning. Today was Monday. Miss Bessie would be getting ready to go to her office in the county courthouse in Bayview.

His early visit would not be a social one. It was a duty, and one the preacher was not looking forward to. Since Carl Hansen's death, the Reverend had been well aware of the two factions at work in the village. It was his duty to try to work them out peacefully.

However, the preacher wasn't feeling very optimistic about Miss Bessie's part in it. Her intentions concerning Carl's granddaughter had been obvious all along. Miss Bessie was a hard, stubborn nut to crack.

On the other hand, the villagers could be a stubborn lot too. He should know. He had lived among them long enough. Respectable people, most of the time. Cheerful, friendly and good-natured, but clannish. They would not tolerate outside interference. They resented the law. Disputes, no matter how serious, were settled among their own. Despite the hardships of the bitter Depression, none had ever asked for charity. When needs arose, their own people took care of them. Taffy Hansen's unfortunate position was no exception. Her grandfather had died, there were no other kin. Because she was one of them, she was their responsibility. They would provide for her.

All this was going through Reverend Hammond's mind when he knocked on the door of the Tyler home. Miss Bessie, dressed in a robe and slippers, appeared.

"I would like a word with you, Miss Bessie," the preacher said casually. "May I come in?"

Miss Bessie looked annoyed. "Uh, yes, Reverend. Come in."

She led the way back to the kitchen, where a lamp burned in the center of a round table.

"I'll come right to the point, Miss Bessie. I know your time is valuable. It's about Taffy Hansen. We're all concerned about her welfare now that Carl—"

Miss Bessie cut him off. "Of course we are, Reverend, but now we can all rest easy. As you may have suspected," she went on, enjoying the role she was playing, "we have many foster homes open to us, but few that come up to our requirements. However, I've been very fortunate to be able to arrange an excellent home for Taffy. It's located in Bayview. A family named Eldredge. I'll take Taffy there tomorrow morning."

Reverend Hammond looked stunned. "You operate with surprising speed, Miss Bessie. But why the rush? Why do you think it necessary to place Taffy so quickly?"

"It's best to get things over with," she snapped.

"Even so, you must be aware of Taffy's grief. Surely you don't believe it's going to help her to throw her into an entirely new environment before she has had a chance to get her feet on the ground?"

"Reverend Hammond," Miss Bessie replied, "I am not accustomed to being told how to proceed with my work.

Must I remind you that I am the agent in charge of this matter? Perhaps you should go back to your duties of the church and let me handle my job as I see it."

The discussion was in shambles. The preacher forced the anger from his voice.

"Let's try to be reasonable," he said calmly. "I came here this morning to see if you would discuss Taffy's case with some of our people here in the village. It stands to reason she would be far better off living among her own kind—"

"For your information," Miss Bessie interrupted, "there are no foster homes in the village listed with our agency. Now, Reverend, if that is all, I'll see you to the door."

The preacher rose to his feet.

"There is more, Miss Bessie. You're right, of course. There are no families from the village listed with your agency, but I have a strong feeling there will be before the day is out. Good Christian families. Financially qualified. Not families seeking payments for their efforts, but offers made from the goodness of their hearts. Judge Harrison will be petitioned. Think about it, Miss Bessie, before you decide to whisk Taffy away tomorrow morning."

Once outside, Reverend Hammond breathed deeply. He walked to the docks at the waterfront, where he saw a light burning in the part of the fish house Mr. Tanner used for an office. Without ceremony, the preacher opened the screen door and let himself in. Most of the room was taken up by an ancient, marred desk. A single light bulb hung on a cord from the ceiling. Mr. Tanner looked up.

"Something has come up, Mr. Tanner."

"Figured that, Reverend. Sit down."

The preacher talked in low, angry tones about the things he had just learned from the welfare agent. As he talked, Mr. Tanner's eyes grew dark with concern. "First thing Reverend, we got to go find Taffy. Make sure she knows how things are. I'll get Jonas. We'll go up to the shack in the launch."

Thunder rumbled overhead as Jonas fired up the engine.

"Going to get some weather," Mr. Tanner announced. "Maybe you better stay here and keep an eye on things till we get back with Taffy." Reverend Hammond was strictly a fair-weather sailor.

As the launch pulled away, the preacher marveled at the way the seasoned boatmen took the weather in stride. Within seconds, the boat was swallowed up in fog.

It seemed an eternity before he heard the muffled sound of the launch returning. When it pulled up at the platform, he could clearly see that Taffy was not aboard.

No one spoke until Mr. Tanner was on the landing.

"She wasn't there, Reverend," Mr. Tanner said. "Jonas and I covered every inch of that place. Most of her clothes were gone. Pantry cleaned out. Vegetable garden stripped down to the last green tomato. Even the cat was gone."

Tight lines around the old man's face gave him a tired, beaten look. He spoke again. "Her skiff is gone, too."

Just then, two young fishermen, finished with their work, walked off the catwalk.

"Toady! Billie Joe!" Mr. Tanner shouted. "Go round up anyone in the village who hasn't already gone fishing. Tell them to get down here right away."

"Yes, sir, Mr. Tanner," one of them said. "But what's going on? What do you want us to tell 'em?"

"The Hansen girl left home in her skiff. Tell the men we're organizing a search party."

"Yes, sir!"

≈ **10** ≈

John Hillard stirred on his bed. He opened his eyes. Through blurred vision he could see rainwater streaming off the shutters outside. He sat up, fumbling for the bottle of wine he always kept on the table beside his bed. And then he remembered. There wasn't any wine. Old Gus had cut him off.

Fool! he thought, groaning aloud. Why had he polished off the whole bottle last night? He gazed mournfully at the empty bottle and ran his hands over his face.

With effort, he sat up and looked about the room. His eyes slowly came to rest on Jody's bed. A thin trickle of water dribbled onto the quilt. On unsteady legs, John stumbled to the kitchen area to find a pan, but all were stacked in the sink, greasy with food. Sagging against the cluttered counter, he hid his face in his hands and sobbed. The morning had hardly begun, and already his nerves were in shambles. How was he ever going to get through the day?

From experience, he knew there was nothing left to do but go down to the docks, look up old Hank, and go back fishing. He looked at Jody's bed again. It was made up like always, with the quilt spread neat and the pillow in place. But where was Jody? He tried to think back to the last time he had seen him, but couldn't remember. It didn't matter, he told himself. Jody was probably around the docks somewhere. He'd find him there.

But when John arrived at the docks, the place was deserted. Even old man Ike, who ran the boat works, and Jonas, who took care of the gas pumps, were gone. Strange, he thought. Where were the fishermen? He had never seen the busy waterfront so quiet. He pulled his raincoat tighter around his neck and wandered back through the village to the tavern.

Gus was there. John hesitated briefly, then stepped inside. "Mornin', Gus," John said lamely. Gus looked up, grinning. "Mornin', John."

John waited silently. Gus wasn't making any move to come up with the usual jug of leftover spirits. When he was cut off, he was cut off all the way.

He edged closer to the counter, eyes first on Gus, then on the bottles lining the back shelf. He stared longingly at the rows of amber and red liquid.

"How about a cup of coffee, John? Just made a fresh pot."

The thought of hot coffee made him feel sick, but he knew he wasn't going to get anything any better. He shrugged. "Yeah, Gus. Guess so."

The tavern keeper poured two cups of coffee.

"Where's everybody at, Gus?"

"Still out on the water huntin' for the Hansen girl. Won't anybody be back 'fore dark." He reached for a towel and began drying glasses.

John gripped the coffee cup in both hands in an attempt to get it to his mouth. It wobbled, spilling coffee over the counter.

"Man, you are in bad shape, now ain't you? When was the last time you had anything to eat?"

John didn't answer. The thought of food made him sick.

Gus watched the shaking hands reach out once more for the coffee. Then, with a resigned shrug, he reached for a bottle of wine and poured a generous amount in a glass. He set it on the counter in front of John. The sick eyes instantly came alive as John stared at the glass in disbelief.

"On me, John. To help you over the hump. But there won't be no more. Drink up and go home. Get yourself straightened up."

"Thanks, Gus, you just saved my life. Now all I have to do is go find old Hank. See about going back fishin'."

"You won't be findin' Hank," Gus said. "Nobody's at the docks. Old Hank, or nobody else. They're out on the water scattered all the way from the gulf to Tally's dam up the river. Lookin' for Taffy Hansen!"

John lowered his eyes and nudged the coffee aside. He reached for the wine.

"By the way, John," Gus went on. "How's Jody's leg coming along? That catfish gouged him good from what Jonas told me."

John's hand hesitated. He knew Gus was waiting for an answer, but he couldn't trust himself to speak. How could he tell Gus that he didn't know anything about Jody's leg?

He sat like someone turned to stone, his face haggard and drawn as shame seared through him. How he needed that drink! It was only inches from his fingertips, yet he was powerless to pick it up. He stared at it like someone in a trance, then bolted for the door.

"Well!" Gus muttered, drawing his heavy brows together. "Now I've seen it all!"

John staggered home like a blind man, wondering what had come over him at the tavern. That wine! Why couldn't he drink it?

Then he knew why. For the first time, he had seen himself as a wasted nobody, someone on a one-way street to hell. One more drink would finish him off. It was as frightening and final as that.

In a cold sweat, John stumbled into the shack and

slumped down in a chair, aware of a foul smell in the room. Where *was* Jody? he wondered. Was he in some kind of trouble? Why wasn't he here? Jody hated a filthy house, John remembered. The boy had once spent time trying to keep it clean but had finally given up.

John looked around. First thing, he thought, was to clean it up. Have it sparkling when Jody came home. At least that would be a step in the right direction.

He set a pail of water on the stove to heat. Might as well get started. He would clean every inch of the hut, scrub all the pots and pans, dig a hole in the backyard and bury the garbage, then scrub the floor until you could eat off it. Jody would be pleased when he got home. John's spirits slowly began to rise.

He reached for the broom and swept furiously, piling rubbish in the middle of the room as he worked. Then, under his own bed, the broom touched an object shoved way back against the wall. He nudged it free. It was a sealed bottle of wine, covered with dust.

The broom slid to the floor with a bang as he stared in awe. He picked the bottle up gingerly, lovingly, dusting it carefully on the sleeve of his shirt. His dismal world had suddenly slipped back into proper perspective.

He hurriedly unscrewed the cap, but when he raised the bottle to his lips, he felt again the same strange promise of doom. He felt that if he tasted that wine on his lips, if one small swallow found its way into his stomach, all hope of reconciliation with Jody would be gone forever. He stared long and hard at the bottle. Muscles tightened into hard knots at the back of his jaw, drawing his mouth into a thin, tight line. He turned away, slowly sinking to his knees in the midst of the trash on the floor. Choking sobs convulsed his body, blinding his eyes, until at last, his body spent and shaken, he lapsed into grim silence.

Slowly his lips began to move. At first no sound came,

then, as if with effort, he spoke in a halting whisper. "Listen, God . . . please. I'm squatted down here on my knees, in the middle of a mess of garbage, so torn up inside I can't stand it, can't go no farther . . ."

His voice broke. Fresh sobs tore at his throat as another wave of hopelessness swept through him. He screwed up his courage and went on. "Guess you know what's eatin' at me. Guess you know all about me and how I been messin' up Jody's life. You been gougin' at my conscience long enough, and me payin' no attention, just goin' right on drinkin' anything I could get my hands on. Well, God, I can't go no farther and that's a fact . . . not without some help . . . your help, God."

By now the bottle of wine on the table in back of him was like something alive, with eyes boring into his back. He swallowed hard. "You know what that bottle is doing to me, God, so please, if you can see your way clear to help me . . ."

His prayer ended. He stayed there, eyes closed, hands folded in front of him. He didn't want to move, but he knew he had to. There was something he had to do. Something very important.

He rose to his feet slowly and turned around to face the table. With eyes drawn into narrow slits, he looked at the wine bottle, knowing fully the relief that its bright contents could bring to his tortured body.

He took a step forward, grabbed the bottle in both hands. He tucked it in the crook of his arm like a football and fled out the door, scattering litter as he went. Then he threw the bottle across the backyard and watched it smash against the trunk of a banyan tree, glass flying in all directions. With a ragged sigh, he turned back to the hut.

≈ **11** ≈

The Sheriff's Department of Palmview County was notified of Taffy's disappearance. Because the department didn't have a patrol boat, the sheriff was relieved to learn that the village fishermen would conduct the water search on their own. For his part, the sheriff agreed to do the search on land. If the girl got out of her boat and stepped ashore, his men would find her.

The search had begun in an orderly fashion. They fanned out in all directions, some going up the river while others sought out the bayous and back regions behind the islands of both Little and Big Placid bays. They gave freely of their time and efforts, even though they knew it meant no money coming in until the search was over. There was no grumbling among them. The only sour note lay in the fact that they all knew *why* she had packed up and left.

It didn't seem possible to the men that the girl could simply vanish, but, as the days dragged on, it became obvious that she had. At the end of the fourth day, Mr. Tanner called the search off.

"Let's face it, boys," he said, his voice heavy with discouragement, "if we haven't found her by now, we're not going to. Too much time has gone by. Not much we can do now, except for you boys to keep your eyes open when you're out there fishin'."

The men stood around, shifting restlessly on their feet,

reluctant to pick up their gear and go home. The failure of the search had not set well with any of them.

"One more thing we're going to try," Mr. Tanner went on. "The preacher, Jonas, and I, we're going to check out Cranes Bog tomorrow. Don't expect to find anything, but we're going in anyway."

Cap't. Nate, Miss Bessie's husband, stepped forward. "I ain't in no sweat to get back to fishin', and Cranes Bog is a big place. I'll be going with you."

Another man stepped forward. He was tall and lean, his hair freshly trimmed. His general appearance was somewhat conspicuous because he had the only clean-shaven face in the group. "Guess I ain't got nobody to feed, Mr. Tanner," John Hillard said. "I'll be going along too."

Mr. Tanner looked John over closely, remembering how he had come to the docks at dawn on the second day of the search, volunteering his services along with the rest of the men. The old man had wondered then, as now, why he had joined up. What was his motivation? What was on his mind?

"Glad to have you along, John."

≈

With three skiffs in tow, the launch slowly drifted to a standstill at the entrance to the swamp. Reverend Hammond would go in with Jonas, Mr. Tanner with John Hillard, and Cap't. Nate Tyler, by choice, would go in alone. Each would work his own section of the swamp, and all would return to their starting place at a given hour. Each carried a horn to be used in the event that one of the crew happened onto something. Although none were expecting to find Taffy in that dismal place, they were eager to get on with the search.

John Hillard, silent and withdrawn, poled the skiff in

a westerly direction while Mr. Tanner sat on the stern seat scanning the waters through a pair of binoculars. The opening through which they had come was already sealed off, locking the two men in the inner sanctums of the timeless swamp.

"Been studying you these past few days, John. Seems like something is chewin' at you. Want to talk about it?"

The unexpected show of interest from the village patriarch brought a sting of tears to John's eyes. "No, sir," he mumbled, keeping his back turned. Silence fell between them again while John poled on. Mr. Tanner put the binoculars aside. He reached in his pocket for his pipe and tobacco, spending a considerable amount of time with it before he spoke again. "How is Jody's leg coming along, John?"

Mr. Tanner's keen eye observed a change come over the younger man. He saw his body tighten, the poling oar go slack in his hands. He turned to face the old man. "To tell you the plain truth, sir, I don't know. Leastways not on my own."

"Go on, John."

"Miss Daisy, she told me a couple of days ago Jody's leg wasn't healin' up right. Said she was worried about him."

Mr. Tanner put his pipe down beside him on the seat. "Tomorrow morning I'll go by and have a look at him, John. Maybe take him back to that doctor in town."

"That's just it, Mr. Tanner. Jody ain't there. He ain't nowhere in the village. Nobody's seen him for nigh onto a week now. His skiff is gone. And most of his gear."

The old man's eyes grew dark. "Why would he do that if his leg was bad?"

A haunted look came into John's eyes. "Can't say for sure, sir, but I got me a gut feeling about it. All that time he was hurtin' so much, I never lifted a finger to help him. Didn't even know anything about it, to tell the

75

truth. Figgered he took off in a huff. Can't blame him any. . . ." John gripped the poling oar and shoved the skiff forward with a jolt. "Got a feeling this time he ain't gonna be coming back."

Mr. Tanner was quiet for a long time. Green islands slid by as John poled past hidden lagoons with herons dotting the flats. Finally, he spoke. "And all this time we were on the search for Taffy, nobody saw anything of Jody."

"No, sir. And I was lookin' for him."

Mr. Tanner ran his fingers through the white wisps of hair covering his head. He scowled into the distance. "Sure don't like the sound of that. Not with Jody's leg messed up. If what you're thinking is true, John, then maybe I better get in touch with that sheriff. Ask him to keep an eye out for Jody, too, just in case. The boy might need some help with that bum leg."

"Yes, sir. And while we're on the subject, I may as well tell you I don't aim to set around doin' nothin' either. I'm goin' back to fishing long enough to pay my bill at Gus's place and Goddard's store and get me a grubstake. Then I'm goin' huntin' for Jody myself."

Mr. Tanner looked up. "What kind of plans you got, John?"

"Figger it this way, sir. Miss Daisy told me what kind of medicine that doctor gave Jody to use on his leg. Peroxide, permanganate—things you don't see much of except in a drugstore. The boy probably took some with him, but sooner or later he might run out and need some more. When he does, he'll have to find a drugstore."

They trailed around one island after another, scanning the waters. Sand flies chewed at them. The rays from the sun burned hotter.

"Been doing some thinking, John," Mr. Tanner said after a while. The old man picked up his pipe and knocked the dead ashes overboard, knowing full well that what he was about to propose could very easily turn out to be a grave mistake. Still, he was going to take the chance. "Maybe we can get together on something."

John sat down and wiped sweat from his face while Mr. Tanner relit his pipe. He looked at the old man through a haze of blue smoke, offering no comment.

"This search you're talking about," Mr. Tanner went on. "Might take a lot more time and effort than you're thinking about. Could get real discouraging."

"I figger on sticking it out, sir. Sooner or later, I'll find something. That boy has to be someplace."

"You're right, John, and so does Taffy Hansen. Suppose, instead of you using your skiff like you was talking about, you was to take my small launch. You could cover more water in a lot less time. And the launch cabin could come in mighty handy in bad weather. And while you're looking for Jody, you could be looking for Taffy, too."

John's eyes opened wide. Still, he made no comment.

"I could stock your launch with grub and furnish you with gas money. Pay your bill at the store and Gus's place. This would be a two-way proposition, John. You go on your search, I'll put up the money."

John was not prepared for what he was hearing. *Someone was actually putting trust in him! Offering assistance. Reaching out to help him!*

For a moment he couldn't speak. He slowly got to his feet and held out his hand. His voice was husky with emotion. "I'll find those two kids, Mr. Tanner. I'll find them both. I won't stop until I do. You can count on it, sir."

≈

The day's search ended at dusk without a shred of evidence that anyone had been in the big swamp since the dawn of time.

≈ 12 ≈

Miss Bessie examined her flock of white leghorns until she found the one she was looking for. She held the chicken under her arm, running her fingers down the smooth feathers until they came to rest between the thighs. Her thin lips pressed tight as she concentrated and probed. Sure enough, the space was much narrower than in the other hens. This one wouldn't be laying for months—it was due for the stewpot.

She tucked the fowl tight under her arm, carried it to a pine stump, pried the hatchet blade out of the wood, and, with one clean chop, took its head off. She turned away, ignoring the blood staining the grass.

This evening she would have a nice supper for Nate— chicken pilaf and fresh collard greens—but she knew nothing would change. Nate would just sit there and eat, keeping his eyes on his plate, refusing to speak to her.

It had all started, of course, with the disappearance of Taffy Hansen. Nate blamed her for the girl's running away, just like everyone else in the village.

She shrugged. They'd get over it sooner or later. Once the search was over, everything would settle down to normal again. Miss Bessie couldn't see what all the fuss was about anyway. The girl had left of her own accord. Maybe she was visiting friends, or had just wanted to get off by herself for a while. In any event, when she came back, she would still end up in the foster home with the Eldredge family.

As she picked up the chicken and dunked it in a pail of hot water, Miss Bessie's thoughts took her back to the time she had first seen Carl Hansen's granddaughter.

It had been shortly after Taffy had arrived in Buttonwood Harbor. The little girl had been in the grocery store with Carl, surrounded by a group of women fussing over her, offering her sweets. Carl had stood by, beaming proudly. The shy, upturned face, framed in ringlets, had glowed softly in the sunlight filtering through the windows.

The burning image of that first encounter was one Miss Bessie would never forget. She had looked at the child, through her, beyond her, to another time, another place. She had seen the face of another child, her own little Jenny, alive again before her eyes. The Jenny she had had for a few short years. Miss Bessie had seen the same light in this little girl's eyes, the same fullness of the mouth, and in that moment something had broken inside her.

Wave after wave of painful memories, so carefully tucked away, had resurfaced. There had been a sudden impulse to gather this child to her, to feel the warmth of the little body pressed close, and in the next instant had come the terrible pangs of resentment. Jenny was dead. Miss Bessie wanted nothing from this child. The striking resemblance between them was a cruel and hideous joke that fate had played on her.

She had endured her torment in silence, confiding in no one. If Nate had seen the resemblance as she had, he'd made no comment. His life had gone on as before, while her own had been painfully changed.

As time had passed, her bitterness had increased. She'd watched the child's steady growth with each passing season and subconsciously calculated the developments of her own little Jenny, had she lived. It had been like living through Jenny's death over and over again.

At times, she had shut herself away in order to avoid a chance encounter with the child. She'd pretended illness, staying away from church for weeks at a time. She'd shopped for groceries in Bayview instead of at the little store in the village. When her confinement became too oppressive, she would venture out again, hoping that the girl would no longer have any effect on her. Hoping that it would be different.

It never was. Sooner or later, their paths would cross. Miss Bessie would settle down in a church pew with Nate, taking in all the things she had missed. She would be at peace with herself. Then she would look up, see Taffy's slender figure walking down the aisle with her grandfather, and the feeling of peace would drain away.

Her thoughts were interrupted when Nora came around the corner of the house. Since Nate wasn't speaking to Miss Bessie, her sister kept her informed of the happenings in the village. "I saw Reverend Hammond this morning, Bessie," Nora said. "He said if they haven't found Taffy by tonight, Mr. Tanner is going to ask for volunteers to go with him on one more search. This time in Cranes Bog."

For the first time in her life, Miss Bessie found herself at a loss for words. She looked up quickly. What was Nora saying? Taffy, in *Cranes Bog*? Now guilt settled over her like a black omen. Cranes Bog! God in heaven!

≈ **13** ≈

Because Jody was already familiar with the waters on the hundred-mile stretch to Pelican Island, he needed nothing other than his marine chart and his memory to get him there. It would be a snap, he reminded himself, just like before, only this time they would travel by night. They would follow the shorelines of the bays and bayous between the offshore gulf barrier islands and the mainland. Poling would be easy. Nothing to hamper their steady pace except the occasional swift-running waters between the barrier islands that emptied out in a fury with each turn of the tide.

Jody had figured four nights out would give them plenty of time to get to their destination. That would amount to five or six hours of poling at a time, leaving the rest of the night free for eating snacks, digging for clams or oysters, and stopping for water and rest periods.

However, there was one thing he hadn't counted on. His leg. His sorry, insufferable leg! When he and Miss Taffy had left the shell bar, Jody had felt sure his leg would be all right. He'd felt better than he had in weeks. The gaping hole had been just as deep as before, but the angry redness of flesh around it had all but disappeared, leaving his skin shiny and pink. It was then that he had decided that there would be no fires along the way to heat water for soakings. Too risky, he had concluded. The sheriff's people would be looking for Miss Taffy.

Notices might be tacked on walls in public places. A girl in a skiff. If Jody was to build a fire on some stretch of beach, it might attract attention. He wouldn't chance it, no matter how much Miss Taffy nagged him.

Jody had managed to push on each night, at least until around midnight, when the ache in his leg had become unbearable. After that came the rest periods, holding up their progress until now he had lost all track of time. How many nights had passed? Five, six? He wasn't sure.

He looked over his shoulder at the moon above. Somewhere around one o'clock, he estimated. His leg was throbbing as it had for the past several hours. He put the pole down and slipped overboard into waist-deep water, working his leg back and forth to break loose some of the infection. Another delay, but this time hope was in sight. The long and grueling trip was almost over. Six or seven miles farther would bring them to the shores of Pelican Island. Before dawn, he would be resting on the warm beach sand, his leg soaking in a pail of steaming hot water.

He glanced back at Miss Taffy, whose boat looked like a dark shadow moving over the water.

Taffy slid her skiff up beside his. "Everything all right, Jody?"

"Yes, Miss Taffy. Just resting."

He crawled back in his boat, but he didn't feel rested. His body felt heavy. He pulled on his shirt and sat on the stern seat. "May as well take a breather, Miss. Another two or three hours and we'll be on Pelican Island."

In the dim light, Jody saw the flash of white teeth. "Oh Jody! I can hardly wait!"

He took his time bandaging his leg, feeling muscles strain with the effort. He stood up, wincing. The night was cool, yet beads of sweat stood out on his body. He reached for the poling oar, convinced the next two hours would be the longest of his life.

"Might as well get going," he said gently.

They shoved on, Jody in the lead. Taffy could barely contain herself. *Seven more miles!* Each push on the oar brought her closer to Jody's island in the gulf. Their home away from home. She felt like calling out to the egrets that sailed by in the moonlight. Seven more miles and they could plant their feet on solid ground again. She would scrounge up firewood. Get Jody's leg soaking. Cook a hot meal. Explore the island at first daylight. She could hardly wait!

She thought about the abandoned house on the point Jody had described, and the small farming community on the mainland called St. Clair. Three miles north of Pelican Island as the crow flies, he had said. Jody had gone there once for supplies. He had talked about the general store, the fish market, the post office, and the farms. Truck farms, pig farms, chicken farms, and, farther inland at the edge of the highway, a gladiolus farm.

In a short time, Jody told her they would leave the bay waters and head out into the Gulf of Mexico. Weather conditions were just right. A dead clam prevailed, lulling all the surface waters into the stillness of a mountain lake. At slack tide they slipped across the sleepy pass, emerging into the crystal clear gulf. Taffy followed Jody into the shallows along the shoreline.

She let the pole trail behind as she looked out over the shimmering vastness of water before her. Moonlight cast an enchanting pathway over the surface. Taffy, of course, had been seeing the same moon all her life, but on this journey there was something different about it. The moon was no longer just a distant object in the sky to be wondered at, but a friendly traveling companion lighting their way. Sleeping by day. Watching over them by night.

After an hour or so, Jody began searching the water offshore, hoping to see the dim outline of Pelican Island. His poling oar felt heavy, and fleeting spells of dizziness came over him. He was breathing air deep into his lungs, but, for some reason, he couldn't seem to get enough of it.

Suddenly an unnerving weakness made him sag forward. He locked his knees to brace himself and, with mounting uneasiness, waited for the weakness to pass.

It didn't. A roaring sound came into his ears, drowning out all other sounds. He took a deep breath, then another. Blackness swarmed in front of his eyes. In his last moment of consciousness, he dropped the poling oar in the bottom of the boat. Total darkness closed in.

Taffy, still preoccupied with the moonlit night, glanced ahead and saw the bulk of Jody's boat. She looked again. His skiff was in plain sight, but she couldn't see Jody. She pushed hard on her pole to catch up, calling out to him. "Jody. . . ."

There was no response. Her boat slid into position alongside his. Jody was in the bottom of the boat, eyes closed. He lay on his side. One arm was draped over the side railing, the other was hidden under his body. Even in the shadow, Taffy could see that his face was chalk white.

"Jody!" she screamed in panic.

There was no movement.

She looped the stern line through a cleat and scrambled into his skiff. She unbuttoned his shirt, holding her palm to his chest. His heartbeat was slow and steady.

A splash of water in his face brought a flutter to his eyes. He stirred, then looked up at her.

"What's a matter?" He sat up, wiping water from his face.

"Jody! What happened? What's wrong?"

"Don't know . . . exactly. I felt dizzy. Then, all of a sudden, I was down here in the bottom of the boat." He leaned on the railing to support his weight as he slid onto the stern seat. "I'm all right now, Miss Taffy. I feel better. Just a little shaky. Nothin' to worry about. I'll just rest up a minute and we can go on."

Taffy came to her feet slowly. There was an angry edge to her voice when she spoke. "That's all you've said since we left the swamp, Jody. 'Nothin' to worry about.' When are you going to stop acting like nothing's the matter and start facing facts?"

Jody's face emptied out like he had been struck. He stared up at her. Until now, not one cross word had passed between them.

"Your leg is in awful shape again, Jody," she went on, her voice shrill with the fear she was feeling, "but you wouldn't build a fire so you could soak it. So what if somebody had seen us? We could have fibbed about who we are and where we came from, then moved on. But no, not you. Just made us push on like it was the only important thing in the world.

"Scared me half to death, you passing out like that. My heart is still racing around like crazy, and you settin' there telling me there's nothing to worry about!"

Her voice faltered. Tears came to her eyes. "There's plenty to worry about. You need a doctor . . . I'm scared, Jody," she sobbed.

Jody came out of his stunned silence. "You know I can't go to a doctor." He hung his head. "Guess you'd be better off without me. Least that way you wouldn't be stuck with a cripple."

Taffy sat down beside him. She lifted his chin, forcing him to look at her.

"It's not like that, Jody," she said, "and I don't ever want you to say that again. I'm not stuck with a cripple. It's your stubbornness I'm stuck with. If you're not going to take care of yourself and red streaks start going up your leg, I'll have to find somebody in St. Clair to haul you to a doctor, and the authorities will have us back in Buttonwood Harbor before we know what's happening.

85

We're in this together. So stop saying everything is all right and start thinking about the seriousness of your infection."

Jody's eyes were like two dark pools. "All right," he mumbled, "but there's not much I can do about it now."

"Yes, there is," she countered. "You can start by staying off your leg for the rest of the way to Pelican Island." She reached for the folded quilt lying on top of his gear and laid it over the stern seat while Jody squirmed around to make room.

"Now lie down. I'm going to tow you the rest of the way. I'll go on like we been going, following the shore until you tell me when to head out to your island."

Jody didn't protest. He settled on the quilt, dangling his injured leg overboard. He closed his eyes.

Taffy looked down at the still pale face in the moonlight. A shock of dark hair lay over his forehead. He was like a little boy. She reached down to touch his cheek.

"Feeling better, Jody?"

Jody didn't answer. He had fallen asleep.

≈ **14** ≈

Bright noonday sun glinted off the cabbage palms on Pelican Island and spilled over new stalks of budding sea oats lining the bluff. It warmed the white sand where Taffy stood, and sparkled over the gulf waters beyond. Taffy shaded her eyes against the glare and looked out over the blue-green water. In the distance, she could see the strip of beach on the mainland merging with the tangled jungle beyond, and, farther up the coast, the tiny patch of royal palms towering above the rest of the trees, indicating the location of the little settlement of St. Clair. Nothing moved in the stillness of the day except the gentle stirrings of the coconut fronds overhead. No signs of life marred the tranquillity of the scene. Except for the forlorn old house in back of her, she might have been a castaway on a remote island in the middle of an ocean.

Why then, she wondered, had a feeling of uneasiness dogged her since dawn this morning? Why had she found herself looking over her shoulder all the time? Had she spent too much time in hiding to feel free to move about in the open now?

She turned to look at the wide apron of white sand composing the north end of the island, and the curving arc of shore sweeping to the lee side where she was standing. Nothing grew for a span of several hundred yards, then there was an outcropping of sea oats that merged with the jungle beyond. Backed up beside a vine-covered patch of cabbage palmettos stood the house. A gentle slope of beach led down to the water's edge, where a rickety dock jutted out from shore. Underneath the sagging structure, safely hidden from view, were the two skiffs. Jody slept in the sand nearby. He was lying on his back, with a straw hat covering his face.

Taffy looked back at the old house, knowing she could not be comfortable making camp on this part of the island. She and Jody were too exposed. It was obvious there was no one living within miles of here, but, even so, she reasoned, it was inevitable that a boat would pass sooner or later. Perhaps others knew about the pitcher pump and would stop for water. A camper might come to explore. Anything was possible, and these were possibilities she was unprepared to face at this point. She needed more time to find out for herself just how far from home she was.

She remembered a lagoon on the lee side of the island Jody had talked about. A lagoon sounded a lot more like the kind of a place where she could feel comfortable. She would talk to Jody about it as soon as he awakened.

A crunching sound of dry leaves behind her brought her heart up in her throat. She whipped around. Tar Baby was slowly picking his way through the underbrush where he had been sleeping. He blinked his eyes in the sunlight.

"Come on, Tar. Let's go look inside that old house."

Until now, she had had little time for exploring. She and Jody had arrived at the island an hour before day-break, and Taffy had been busy taking care of Jody ever since. He was still weak, but the spells of dizziness had passed. He had been like a submissive little boy, his solemn, dark eyes always on her as she went about preparing his water and food. After eating, he had fallen asleep.

Now, with the cat at her heels, Taffy picked her way through the sea oats and sandspurs until she stood at the foot of the sagging steps leading up to a porch at the front of the house. A screen door hung by one hinge. She slipped through it. The porch was bare except for two wooden benches along the back wall. Fine white sand covered the floor. She opened the door to the main part of the house. Mustiness filled the air.

"Come on, Tar," she said in a half whisper. "Get your nose working in case there's a snake in here."

She stepped cautiously into the dimness of a spacious room. Rows of dingy casement windows on two sides hung thick with cobwebs. Benches lined the walls, but the structure that caught her attention was an enormous travertine fireplace that took up most of the far wall. Under the covering of dust, she could see the pale colors of the limestone showing through. Recesses had been carved into the stonework, and someone had placed a pink murex, a weathered piece of driftwood, and scatterings of coral in them. Her eyes lingered as she thought about the hidden beauty that could be brought to life with a scrub brush and a pail of soapy water.

It was when she reached out to caress the mantel with her fingertips that she noticed the painting hanging on the wall above. The scene was of a great white heron peering into sea green water where it stood against a backdrop of mangroves. So lifelike was the bird that, despite the cobwebs, one might expect at any moment to see a slender olive yellow leg lift to take a step.

Standing on tiptoe, Taffy wiped away a cobweb at the lower part of the painting. There, in fine letters at the bottom right-hand corner, was the artist's name—*J. J. Audubon, Indian Key, 1832*—and, in the bottom center in bold print, ANGEL OF THE SWAMP.

Taffy stood still, staring in awe. John J. Audubon, the great naturalist painter! Her grandfather had admired

Audubon's work. And here was a hundred-year-old original, right in front of her. She couldn't believe it!

"Why?" she asked herself. "Why would anyone leave a treasure like this in an old abandoned house?"

She couldn't take her eyes away. Had the owner forgotten about it when he'd picked up his belongings and left? Had he expected to return one day to claim it? Why hadn't thieves taken it away? Had they not seen the great artist's inscription or recognized the unusual brilliance of color beneath the cobwebs?

A sudden urge came over her to take the painting, but reasoning told her that was not practical. She had no way of storing it out of the weather. Besides, it didn't belong to her. It had been there, undisturbed, for a long time. It was safe enough for now.

She reluctantly turned away to take up her inspection of the rest of the house.

Doors to three bedrooms stood ajar. Each had a bare mattress on a wooden bed, a handmade dresser, and a closet in one of the walls. Outside shutters held the rooms in semidarkness. Just for an instant, Taffy wondered what it would be like to sleep in a real bed once again.

The kitchen stood off to one side. Her eyes swept over the countertops, cupboards, and a two-burner kerosene stove. Out of the corner of her eye she glimpsed a long-legged spider slowly working its way along a bare wall, a bulging white egg sack showing prominently under its body.

Back in the living room, Tar Baby was sitting in the middle of the floor, pawing at the carcass of a dead roach.

"Let's go, Tar."

≈

The shoreline on the east side of the island hung thick with mangroves that extended all the way to the south pass. The early afternoon sun cast a small rim of shadows over the water where Taffy was poling. Jody and Tar Baby sat on the bow.

"If there's an opening to a lagoon in this place, I don't see how you would ever know it, Jody. All the way down the shoreline is nothing but mangroves."

"It's just a little ways farther down, Miss Taffy. See where that water is rippling the surface? That's where the opening is. The tide's going out."

Taffy poled on. She could see the ripple of water emptying out, but she couldn't see any opening to a lagoon.

"It's covered over with branches. There ain't no opening showing."

"Oh."

"You're gonna like it, Miss Taffy, hidden back in there like a little world all by itself. No gumbo or muck layin' round on shore either. It's close enough to the pass to bring in clean water all the time. I happened on it one time when I was poking around. Saw the swash and went in to investigate."

Water around the hidden opening was considerably deeper than along the rest of the shallow shoreline. Broken shells and small pieces of rock lay scattered over the white bottom.

"Right here, Miss Taffy," Jody spoke up. "You have to go overboard and pull the boat through."

Taffy eased into water up to her shoulders and cautiously made her way in. Branches closed in around her, scraping over the boat. She kept her eyes on the clear white bottom, careful to avoid the barnacle-encrusted roots hanging in the water at the sides of the narrow swash. Sunlight showed through the foliage ahead, and then she was staring at a sea green body of water shining in the full sun like polished glass. The lagoon curved out to form a circle, flanked on one side by tall Australian pines, a rim of mangroves on the other. All traces of the light breeze vanished. Even the pines edging up to the beach hung limp in the stillness. In that moment, as her eyes took in the lush scene before her, she knew the perfect hiding place had been found.

She looked back at Jody. "You're really something."

Jody's eyes lit up. "We can build a lean-to up under them pines to get out of the weather. Find some two-by-fours in that lumber pile up at the house, and I can make the rest out of palmetto fans. Tomorrow I'll start looking—"

Taffy cut him off. "Not so fast, Jody. You promised to stay off your leg, at least until the wound closes. I'm not going to be having any more scares like I had last night— and that's that!"

Jody dropped his eyes. "Yes, ma'am."

"Like you said, Jody, we need the lean-to." Her voice was low, gentler. "You know how to make it?"

"Yes," he answered dully. "Good enough, I reckon."

"Then we'll build it together. You be the boss. You can tell me what to do because I don't know where to begin. I'll do the legwork. All right?"

"Guess so."

Taffy looked at the hunched figure on the bow. He was like a little boy again.

"We'll work as a team, Jody. Each doing a job. There's all kinds of important things you'll be doing without putting a strain on your leg. Like measuring the lumber and sharpening the tools and curing the palmetto fans, all the time showing me how to put up the lean-to."

Jody was listening, saying nothing.

"Besides that, I bet you can get some bait and throw your handline right out from shore and catch fish anytime you want to. After all, somebody has to do it."

A sparkle crept back into Jody's eyes. He grinned. "Yeah. Reckon I can."

≈ **15** ≈

Taffy straightened up from her kneeling position on the pine-needle floor of the newly constructed shelter where she was working. She looked with satisfaction at the neat stack of folded clothes on the shelf in front of her. A sweet smell of fresh-cut palmetto fans still hung in the air, mingled with spicy odors of pine coming through the open shutters from outside. She picked up the last canvas bag at her feet and continued with her unpacking.

The lean-to, hidden under the dense Australian pines, had been erected with a lot less strain than she had expected. It was a crude, inelegant structure, but one that suited her and Jody's needs to a tee. The shelter would withstand wind and rain and be cool and dry, and far more comfortable, than anything either of them had had since leaving the village.

The first step had been to cut the palmetto fans and spread them on the ground in single rows with two-by-fours laid across to press them flat. Each day while Taffy transported lumber from the old house, Jody turned over the fans so that the curing process would be uniform. By the time the framework was up, the fans were ready. The small collection of nails Jody had brought with him had to be used sparingly, so he secured the fans to the framework with tough grapevines. When it came to improvising, Jody always had an answer.

"We need hinges for the shutters, Miss Taffy," he had

said. "Gotta have air coming through. And we need a door with canvas on it to keep the rain out. See if you can dig up an old tire or a piece of leather up there at the house."

There were no tires, but she found an old razor strop in the kitchen. Jody soaked it in kerosene and cut it into lengths to make sturdy hinges.

The shelves, hanging flush with the thatched walls from overhead two-by-fours, were his idea too. He made them from the dry, fibrous stalks of the yucca plant and held them in place with more vines.

The last thing in the canvas bag that Taffy unpacked was an old pair of Jody's sneakers. She shook out the sand and straightened the laces, pulling the tongues into place. She set them on the shelf with the rest of his things and stepped back to inspect her handiwork. The shelf next to it held her own personal belongings, and a third one had been set aside for the food supplies. She smiled. Everything was in place.

All at once a cloud passed over her face. She turned back to Jody's shelf. Clean rolls of bandages lay in a neat stack beside his clothes, along with the permanganate crystals. But where were his bottles of peroxide?

Taffy was certain she had sorted through everything to be stored inside. Had she missed one of the canvas bags? She went outside under the trees and lifted the tarpaulin that covered the rest of the gear. There were cooking utensils, lanterns, and jugs of kerosene. There was the canvas bag that held an assortment of sparkling, odd-shaped glass bottles, each piece carefully wrapped in cloth. Taffy reminded herself to ask Jody about these at the next opportunity, but, for now, where was the peroxide? Frown lines deepened in her face. Had Jody used it all and not told her? Could this, then, have something to do with the listlessness she had noticed in him lately? His lack of interest in food?

94

Taffy went back over the few weeks they had been on the island. To all outward appearances, Jody had recovered from the bad spell on the water when he had passed out. He had been taking good care of himself, soaking his leg regularly, and staying off it. When the lean-to first got under way, he had been full of enthusiasm, alert and eager with new ideas, but, as time went on, he'd seemed to lose interest.

She went down to the beach. Jody was in water up to his armpits, slowly moving in a routine that would take him the full length of the lagoon and back before he finished. She called out to him. "Where are you keeping your peroxide, Jody? I can't find it anywhere."

Even from where she stood, Taffy could see a troubled look pass over Jody's face. He didn't answer.

"Where is your peroxide, Jody?" she repeated.

"I ran out," he answered woodenly, averting his eyes.

Taffy's heart sank. She stared in frustrated exasperation at the slat-thin figure before her. "Why didn't you tell me?" she asked in a barely audible voice.

Jody hung his head. "I didn't know what to do."

Taffy's first reaction was to rail out at him, but the look of misery on his face stopped her. Besides, some of it was her own fault for not paying closer attention. Of course he hadn't known what to do. It was inconceivable that Jody, in his condition, could pole all the way to St. Clair to get his peroxide. It was equally inconceivable that he would ask her to do it. Still, one thing was clear: *He had to have it!*

Instead of anger, it was a time for some very serious thinking.

A silence fell between them as Taffy searched for a solution. Jody, in the meantime, was having some uncomfortable thoughts of his own. Now that Miss Taffy had found out about his peroxide, he was sure she would stop at nothing to see that it was replaced. He was the only one to go and get it, but with those miserable spells of weakness sneaking up on him, he wasn't at all sure how he was going to do it. Three miles there and three miles back! Cripes!

Just then Taffy spoke up. "I have an idea, Jody."

Jody hesitated, fully expecting Miss Taffy to announce she would make the trip herself.

"We'll both go. I'll pole us over there and stay in the boat while you go on up to that store. We'll start out tomorrow morning right after breakfast."

"Yeah, Miss Taffy," Jody said, a smile coming over his face. "And you just gave me an even better idea. Instead of going over there straight like the crow flies, we can follow the mainland shoreline. Before we get to the village, you can get out of the boat and wait for me in the sea oats till I come back. That way, nobody will know anything about you."

"All right," she said thoughtfully. "How much walking will you have to do to get to that store?"

"Not much. It's not far from shore. I'll wear long pants so my bandages won't show. Gee, Miss Taffy, that's going to work out just great!"

≈

Later, when the sun was hanging over the tops of the pine trees, Taffy gathered up the water jugs and climbed in her skiff to pole up to the house for water. When she returned, she would wash out Jody's long pants and shirt. After all, he had to look presentable to go into the village tomorrow.

She slid overboard when she came to the exit leading out of the lagoon. Slipping under the mangroves, she pulled the boat behind her as she made her way out. It would have been a simple matter to cut a trail through the branches, but, to ensure against detection, nothing had been disturbed.

Once she was outside, a fresh breeze from the west brought a pleasant coolness to her wet body. She crawled back in the boat and poled on, thinking about Jody and the trip they would make tomorrow. He had been genuinely pleased with the idea of them going together, almost as if it was a kind of outing. And why not? she reasoned. After all, he had been confined to the lagoon these past few weeks. She smiled, remembering one of the few times he had gone with her to the house. It was during the early stages of building the lean-to, when Jody had been feeling better. The sun had begun to set behind the house, and Taffy had just hauled the last two-by-four down to the boat when she had heard Jody shouting excitedly. "Bull reds, Miss Taffy. A whole school of 'em. Just off the dock!"

Taffy had looked where Jody pointed. Sure enough. The water had been black with big redfish.

"See if you can get me some ghost crabs for bait," he had yelled, fumbling under the bow for a handline.

She had scooped up a handful of wet sea grass and set off down the beach at a trot, eyes alert for a glimpse of a long-legged, snow white crab running over the sand. There was only one way to catch a ghost crab. Outrun it before it got to its hole, then pounce on it with sea grass and hold tight so the nimble little claws couldn't pinch.

At the beginning, Taffy had not shared Jody's enthusiasm. She was worn out and wanted to get back to the lagoon. They didn't need any more fish. But Jody's excitement had soon gotten the better of her. She had run down ghost crabs for two hours that night while Jody'd hauled in one bull red after another. It had been a night he would remember for a long time. In fact, the whole thing had had a profound effect on him. He could talk of little else. When the excitement had worn off, he had looked at the practical side. It bothered him to catch good, salable fish and have to turn them back. That night, Jody had brought in at least a dozen redfish, not one running under ten pounds. A hundred or more pounds in two hours of fishing time.

There was a fish market in St. Clair, he reminded her. He was sure he could sell them to the man up there.

Taffy had been thinking the same thing, but she knew it wasn't possible at this time. She had to remind Jody that he would have to be patient until he was stronger. Still, it was something to think about. A way to make money. A way to replenish the food stock.

She was just rounding the last bend in the shoreline, bringing her into clear view of the house, when she looked up and saw the rowboat bobbing in the light chop. It was approximately one hundred yards off the dock. With adrenaline pouring into her bloodstream, she slipped back into a covering of mangroves. The figure manning the oars had his back to her. He was wearing a white T-shirt. His head was bare. She watched as the wet blades dipped in and out of the water with maddening precision, bringing the intruder closer and closer to their island while her stomach twisted into knots.

≈ **16** ≈

With Miss Taffy gone to the house, Jody, in water up to his shoulders, decided it would be a good time to go the full length of the lagoon and look over his glass bottles. He had hidden them in the sand dunes and made a point of looking at them only when Miss Taffy wasn't around. She was too practical. She would expect him to have more worthwhile things on his mind than fooling around with old bottles.

Jody grinned to himself. Sometime within the next month or so, when all his glass was "cured" with that special combination of sun and white sand, he would show each piece to her and see what she had to say. As always, the thought sent an exhilarating flush of pleasure all the way to his toes.

He glanced toward shore. Tar Baby, ears alert and tail swishing, followed, stopping occasionally to swat at a fiddler crab or race up the beach to scare off a covey of sandpipers.

"Come on, Tar, let's race," he called, laughing at his own joke. In his condition, he couldn't race a box turtle.

The beach at the far end of the lagoon was sprinkled with runners of morning-glory vines flaunting their vivid green leaves and lavender blossoms over the white sand. Sea oats and dunes loomed in the background.

Jody's collection of bottles were just as he had left them, neatly laid out in rows over the crest of a dune. He sat down beside them, staring in fascination as his keen eyes picked up the faint traces of coloring that were beginning to bring charm and elegance to each piece.

There was nothing ordinary about his bottles. Each had been hand-picked over a long period of time. Some had been found while rummaging through garbage dumps, others he had found floating in the water. When he left home, he had had to leave the bulk of his collection behind, bringing only the most prized pieces.

He picked up a small hip flask, shaped like a clam. He had found that one floating in Charlotte Harbor.

"Blue!" he squealed in delight, holding it up to the sun for closer examination. Subtle tints of ice blue distinctly showed in the depths of the clear glass.

Jody's eyes danced with pleasure. There was no question about it. His clam was going to be as bright blue as the gulf waters!

"Just look at this stuff, Tar," he exclaimed breathlessly, making a wide sweep of his arm. "Everything is turnin' colors!"

He picked up a six-sided vinegar cruet and a squatty little beer bottle with a flared bottom. Both showed light tones of amber. A handsome decanter with a glass stopper was turning a clear charcoal gray. One of the little ridged perfume bottles was going to be green. A pale sea green!

His eyes came to rest on the bottle he prized most of all: a clear wine bottle shaped like a round blowfish covered with delicate spines. There were flared fins at the sides, and scales, gills, and eyes molded into the glass. From the very first day Jody had seen it on Miss Daisy's mantel, he knew he had to have it. One day, he had screwed up enough courage to ask her if she would give it to him in exchange for cleaning her duck pens for a week.

Miss Daisy had broken out laughing.

"Been trying to figure out what to do with that for a long time," she'd said, handing it to him. "I'm tired of dusting it."

Jody kept the fish bottle by itself, wrapped in layers of cloth to keep it safe, and, when he'd loaded his boat to leave home, he'd stashed it under the stern seat in a cardboard box filled with crushed newspapers. Miss Taffy hadn't found it when she'd gone through his gear. She didn't know anything about it.

He looked at it now. This one was going to be a different color from any of the others. It was showing definite tints of soft, pale lavender. Jody held it reverently in his hands. Surely, if Miss Daisy could see it now, she would want it back!

He looked over his collection again, feeling a deep sense of pride. He didn't want to leave, but there were things he had to do before Miss Taffy got back.

Before he had come to the dunes, Jody had caught three flounder and cleaned them on the flat slab of rock jutting out from shore. He had tied the heads and backbones together and strung them out in the water, knowing that if a blue crab was anywhere in the lagoon, the bait would lure it up. Now Jody was ready. His dip net and pail were already laid out onshore.

He carefully turned over each piece of his glass, then slid backward down the dune. The cat ran on ahead, heading for the rock slab. Tar Baby knew all about blue crabs. Jody caught them almost every day. If any were hanging around the fish heads now, Jody would know about it. The cat's tail would twitch furiously while he paced the rock.

When Jody finished crabbing, he had caught four. He was ready to start dinner. The coals were just right for frying the fish, and, off to one side, the smudge hearth—used to discourage mosquitoes and sand flies—was ready to light.

Jody looked around the lagoon. Dusk was closing in fast. It would be dark in another ten minutes. Where was Miss Taffy?

He felt uneasy. What could have detained Miss Taffy? Had she had trouble getting the pump started? It wasn't like Miss Taffy to dawdle around after dark. She had never been this late before.

He banked the dying coals with wet sea grass and limped down to the water's edge, where his skiff lay at anchor. Pulling the boat behind him, he headed for the opening of the lagoon.

It was nearly dark when he got to the outside. All he could see were the tops of the mangroves silhouetted against a purple sky. Mosquitoes buzzed around his head as he made his slow trek through the water in the direction of the house. He slid his feet on the bottom to keep from stepping on a stingaree. Then, somewhere in the distance, he heard the first sound of a poling oar scraping the side of a boat. He stood still, listening.

"Miss Taffy," he called anxiously.

There was no response. Seconds later, the skiff slid up silently beside him.

"Cripes, Miss Taffy," Jody began nervously. "I been—"

"Get in, Jody," Taffy ordered in a ragged half whisper. "And keep your voice down. There's a man up there . . . up there in a boat. He's . . ." Her voice trailed off while Jody, still in waist-deep water, stood in stunned silence.

"I . . . I never got to the pump. That man in the boat . . . I hid in the mangroves. He never saw me. He unloaded his gear and went in the house like he was fixin' to stay!"

For a moment neither of them spoke. Taffy sat down heavily on the head cap. Tears glistened on her cheeks.

"What do we do now, Jody?" she lamented.

Jody had no answer. He was totally unprepared for the things Miss Taffy had said. He needed time to think.

"That feller up there, Miss Taffy," he began thoughtfully, "did you get a good look at him?"

"Yeah. He was tall and husky. Maybe seventeen or eighteen years old."

"What kind of gear was he unloadin'?"

Taffy thought a moment. She had positioned herself so that she could take in the whole scene, but while it was taking place, the thing uppermost in her mind had been the fact that the intruder was cutting off their water supply. She forced herself to go back over the details.

"He took a reel pole out of his boat. A little dinky one. And I saw him take out a canvas carrying bag with handles on it. That was about all."

"No gigs or cast nets or other fishin' gear?"

"No."

By now the mosquitoes were digging into Jody's shoulders. He splashed water over his body, tied the skiffs together, and climbed in Taffy's boat. She picked up the poling oar.

"Seems like our biggest worry right now is gettin' to the pump, Miss Taffy. We'll have to keep an eye on that feller. Spy on him and find out what he's up to."

He looked at her searchingly. "Think you can cut a trail through the woods up to the house?"

"Guess so. Least that way I can fill the water jugs once in a while when he's not around. But, Jody, what about your peroxide? What can we do about that?"

"I been thinkin'. From what you saw of the gear that guy was packing, I got a hunch he ain't gonna be hanging round here very long. He has all the earmarks of a city feller. What can he do with a flimsy little reel pole? The kind of fish he'll be tying into off that dock will tear up his tackle first thing. And if that doesn't discourage him, the mosquitoes, sand flies, sandspurs, and poison ivy will. Just wait and see."

≈ **17** ≈

Cutting a trail through the woods turned out to be more of a job than Taffy had thought. In the beginning, her intentions were to hack a narrow path in a direct line from the lagoon to the house, leaving about fifty feet at the end undisturbed so the stranger wouldn't see the path.

But it didn't turn out that way. She was just getting started, hacking at palmetto fans, Spanish bayonets, and trailing vines, when the terrain gave way to an unexpected tangle of mangroves. They were thriving in a low place. She skirted the area, veering west, forced to make the trail longer than she had wanted. The work was tough. Wasps, sharp spines, and poison ivy plagued her. But the urgency of the dwindling water supply spurred her on. The job took two full days to complete, but, in the end, the hardship paid off. The path made getting the water—and spying—easy.

It didn't take her long to find out that the intruder was spending a lot of time away from the house. Each morning, he got in his boat and rowed to St. Clair. The first time she saw this, she raced back to the lagoon to gather up the empty water jugs. In relays, she carried them to the pump, filled them, then placed the full jugs along the trail to lug back in her own time.

The stranger usually returned around noon to wile away the day fishing from the dock. At times, Taffy would see him struggling with his reel pole bent almost double with a pound-and-a-half sheepshead. Other times, he would strip down to his drawers and swim. A city guy, just like Jody had said. His torso and legs were white. Surely the mosquitoes were having fun with him!

Sometimes, at low tide, he would row out to the grass flats to hunt for scallops. Taffy knew the little blue-eyed sea creatures were still too small for harvesting, but the city guy picked them up and tossed them in his boat anyway. Then, when he finished, instead of shucking them out, he would get in his boat and head for St. Clair again.

"Do you suppose that house belongs to somebody in his family?" Jody asked one evening.

"Might be, but if it does, he's not doing anything about fixin' it up."

Jody brightened. "Then he ain't aiming on hangin' around."

"I was thinking about something," Taffy said pensively. "He does his cooking outside. All I ever see him eat is fish."

Jody pondered this for a moment. "You think maybe he's down on his luck?"

"Kinda looks that way. He never opens a can of beans or cooks any vegetables, and I've never seen him with a sandwich or an apple. Just fish, cooked on a grate over his fire. But, Jody, why would he come here? It's plain to see he's not suited to this kind of a place. All he knows is how to row his boat and catch a sheepshead or trout once in a while. Nothing he does falls into any kind of a pattern. If he came here to scrounge out a living from the water, he's doing an awful poor job of it."

There seemed to be no explanation, yet the intruder stayed on, subsisting on his daily rations of grilled fish. Taffy's nerves were wearing. The shadows beneath Jody's eyes were an ever-present reminder that things had to change. Something had to be done about Jody's peroxide!

Each day added more resentment as the stranger kept Taffy from things she should be doing. Before he had arrived, she had sieved daily for coquinas—bright-colored little clams no bigger than grapefruit seeds that thrived by the thousands in the surf. She boiled them to make a broth that added flavor to just about everything she cooked. Also, the loggerhead turtles had begun to come up on the gulf beach at night to lay eggs. What a welcome change it would be if Jody could stuff his mouth with some of those! But, because of the intruder, Taffy could do nothing about these things without leaving her footprints all over the beach. All she could do was wait.

One moonlit night she picked up a croaker sack and headed out of the lagoon on foot. "Keep the coals going, Jody," she called over her shoulder. "We'll have roasted clams when I get back."

She slipped under the dark, overhanging mangroves at the exit to the lagoon and stood on the outside, looking at the scene stretching out before her. With the tide at its lowest level, the grass flats on the lee side of the island lay exposed like a manicured lawn gleaming in the moonlight. Taffy could have waded to the mainland shore in water no more than halfway to her knees.

There was no scarcity of clams in the bay waters of Pelican Island, and that night she filled her sack with as many as she could drag back. What they didn't eat they could bed out in the lagoon for future use. She was back in less than an hour.

The next day she came back from her spying to report more news. "He's out there right now on the gulf side with a homemade sieve and a croaker sack spread out on the sand. I watched him fill the sieve with shell and shake it over his sack for an hour or more. What's he doing, Jody?"

"Gosh, Miss Taffy, I don't know," Jody answered thoughtfully, "unless he's messin' around with cup shells maybe."

"Cup shells?"

"Those little white shells that wash up on the beach, no bigger than the head of a match. Sold in shell shops. The tourists make things out of 'em."

"You think he's going to find any?"

"Guess so, if he hunts for 'em at the high-water mark." Jody's voice was unusually quiet. "They're everywhere on the beach, more in some places than others, but they're an awful job to sort out."

Taffy's eyes darkened with aggravation as the possibilities of the intruder's new project began to unfold.

"It figures, Jody. Somebody told him about those cup shells, and now he's trying to get some to sell."

Jody looked downright mournful. "I can't say for sure, Miss Taffy, but it looks that way."

The next few days passed. The intruder continued with his work, sieving and hauling shell during the day, spending long hours in the evening sorting.

Jody was as upset about the new development as Taffy. That meddler up there at the house was going to go on fooling with cup shells sure as anything, he concluded. In the meantime, the infection in his leg sent little reminders to bug him: the weakness, the dizziness, his inability to help things along. He had already stepped up his hot water soakings. It seemed like he was forever in a prone position with his leg stuck in a pail of water. Or out in the lagoon. His skin was always wrinkled.

Jody knew now his leg was not going to heal. Not the way it was going. Miss Taffy was right. He needed peroxide. If that guy up there didn't clear out soon, then Jody would have to come up with something, and whatever it was couldn't wait much longer.

≈ **18** ≈

Jody sat in the edge of the water cleaning the meat out of a horse conch he had just finished boiling. Stickiness oozed down his hands as he gripped the tough mass of red muscle. Gently pushing the meat from side to side, he felt the muscle breaking away as the suction inside the tight coils loosened. He continued to tug, ever so gently so as not to break any of the soft membrane inside, until at last the whole internal part dropped out in his hand, intact.

He held the impressive-looking bulk, marveling, as he always did, at the handsome spiral structure of the membranes. Each coil lay smoothly over the next, diminishing in size to a tiny tip at the apex, the exact shape of the shell it had inhabited. To Jody, there was nothing repulsive about it.

He dug into his pocket and produced a piece of cord. Tying it around the blob, he secured it to the slab of rock lying in the edge of the water. The conch meat was going to attract a lot of crabs before the day was out.

The job, so easy, brought on another wave of weakness. Beads of sweat popped out on his forehead. He unwound himself from his sitting position in the water and, on hands and knees, crawled back to shore. He stretched out on his back, covering his face with his hat, willing the despair he was feeling to go away. He promptly fell asleep.

Sometime later Jody struggled to bring himself awake, but something held him back, prolonging the cold fear brought on by a dream. He was staring at his leg and seeing only a bare bone between his ankle and his knee. The stark illusion floated before him, and he screamed in terror, yet he knew no sound came from his lips.

A light crunch of footsteps behind him brought Jody fully awake. He turned his head, expecting to see Miss Taffy returning from the house. Instead, he looked into the face of a total stranger. He shrank back.

"Didn't mean to startle you, fella. The name's Jeff Evans. I got a whiff of your campfire and came to investigate. I'm camping in that old house up there on the point."

The friendly, easy manner of the guy was disarming. Jody liked the husky voice, the ready smile and flash of white teeth in the recently sunburned face. Yet he could not bring himself to speak.

So this was the city guy who was messing everything up! He sneaked a glance over at the smoldering campfire a short distance away. The wind had died out, and a stream of smoke was going straight up. The guy had seen it from the gulf side and worked his way right into their lagoon!

This was the last straw!

Still, he seemed a decent enough sort, Jody conceded. Big, capable-looking, and friendly. For an instant, Jody had an impulse to reach out to him, to trust him. He stared up at him, barely drawing a breath. Then Jody's mind cleared. Of course he couldn't confide in this stranger. He shouldn't even give his right name.

The seconds ticked by. Jody set his jaw and lifted his eyes. Jeff's smile was still in place. Jody heard himself speaking in a voice he barely recognized. "Jamie . . . Jamie Thomas. Camping out."

≈ **19** ≈

Frown lines deepened in Taffy's face with each loud creaking sound that came out of the old pump. The racket would wake the dead, she thought irritably, working the handle while she cupped her other hand around the spout of an earthen jug. But at least the city guy wouldn't hear it: He was too far away. She had watched him with his sieve and pails go around the point, then on farther to where he began his work. She was safe for the time being. There was no reason to hurry.

She pressed the cork in the last jug and set out down the trail to haul the water back in relays, thinking about the night before. She had twisted and turned on her quilt, troubled by the conviction that the intruder was not going to leave. He had been on the island ten days, and most of that time had been taken up with cup shells. Obviously, he wasn't going to pull up stakes now. Then, with anxiety weighing heavily on her, she had come up with the possibility of going to St. Clair before daylight and coming back after dark. The more she thought about it, the more she liked the idea. She could slip by the city guy, get Jody's peroxide, and not have to worry anymore. She would set out tomorrow morning, she had decided, while the stars were still bright overhead. She wondered why she hadn't thought of it before.

When the sea green water of the lagoon came into view, Taffy set the jugs down and straightened up, feeling the pull of muscles across her shoulders. She glanced over the water to see what Jody was doing, and froze in her tracks.

The city guy, bare from the waist up, had his back to her. He was talking to Jody, gesturing with his hands while Jody sat like a little bronzed statue, staring up at him.

A strangled cry, starting at the base of Taffy's throat, came out as a muffled gasp of rage. She quickly stepped back into the underbrush, slumping to her knees.

"That detestable . . . contemptuous . . . sneak," she hissed between clenched teeth. How could he have found his way in here? Hadn't she seen him not a half hour ago working with his stupid cup shells on the beach? *How could he!*

She got to her feet and glared across the water, seething with resentment. Poor Jody! How thoroughly miserable he must be, she thought, faced with that guy asking a lot of questions. But Jody was no fool. If asked about the two boats anchored in the water, he would say he was using the second boat to carry his gear. He would be careful to make no mention of her.

Taffy was trying to figure out the best course of action. She could stay where she was until the snoop got tired of talking and went home. He need not know about her. But then what? He still knew about Jody.

She thought about the two of them leaving the island, then promptly dismissed the idea. Jody was in no shape for another venture. And there was nothing to be gained by staying hidden. The snoop would be back. The damage was already done.

She jerked the water jugs up and left the protection of the underbrush. She had no choice but to face the stranger now. While she stomped around the curve of the shore, she thought about how she had planned to pose as a grubby young boy on her trip to St. Clair. She

111

might as well do the same thing now. Two boys camping on a deserted island. There was nothing unusual about that.

The city guy's back was still turned to her, and she saw a startled look cross Jody's face when he saw her.

She came up behind the stranger, set the water jugs down, and, with effort, forced her voice to sound civil. "Howdy, stranger."

The big guy whipped around, obviously startled and momentarily taken aback. A broad grin broke out over his face.

Taffy found herself staring into a pair of warm, friendly eyes. The stranger stared back, appraising her with lively interest and open curiosity.

A quick glance passed between her and Jody, who by now was gaping at her in utter bewilderment. *Why?* his eyes asked.

Taffy extended her hand. "I'm Chris Adams."

"Jeff Evans, ma'am. I'm staying in that house up on the point. Pleased to make your acquaintance."

The powerful hand holding her own felt warm and reassuring, yet Taffy could feel the blood draining from her face while inwardly she recoiled. *Ma'am!* Without so much as a second glance, he had called her *ma'am!*

The tip of her tongue slid nervously over her lips as her last shred of confidence ebbed away. She stared down at her feet.

"Jeff's from Tampa," Jody stammered. "He's leaving tomorrow morning to go back home."

Taffy's heart slid to a standstill. She looked up at Jeff dully. *Leaving the island. Tomorrow morning. God in heaven! Why hadn't she stayed hidden?*

New anger poured through her. Why did everything have to go wrong? Why couldn't she have had just a little more patience? Cripes! What miserable, sorry luck!

All at once she felt old and beaten. Her shoulders

sagged. She stared, speechless, at the person before her, trying hard to hide the bitterness boiling up inside her. The smile was still in place on the stranger's angular, honest face.

"I was just telling Jamie how I hated to leave here and go back to Tampa."

Jamie. She would have to remember.

"You have folks there, Jeff?" Jody asked politely.

"Sure have. A mom and dad and five brothers and sisters. One brother, Andy, just about your age."

"Tell me about him."

Let him talk, Taffy thought grimly. As long as he talked about himself, he wasn't questioning them. It was time she needed, time to try to figure out if anything could be salvaged from the mess she had made of things.

Jeff made himself comfortable in the dry sea grass while Jody plied him with questions. He spoke of his search for work in Tampa and his reason for coming to Pelican Island. He was the oldest in the family, just out of high school, he told them. His folks could use some extra money. There were no jobs to be had in Tampa. He had tried for three summers to find work and finally got into a cafeteria last year washing pots and pans for a dollar a day. It was good while it lasted, he said, but he'd had to give it up when school started. The job was full-time.

Jeff hesitated before going on. "My grandfather built that old cypress house on the point. Years ago, when my dad was just a boy. I always had a special feeling about it. When I couldn't do any good in Tampa, I got the idea to try to find work in St. Clair and live here, but I didn't have any luck with that either. All I can do now is move on and keep looking."

A silence fell between them. Then Jody asked, "Your grandfather built that old house?"

"Yes. He staked out a claim with a land grant from the

government and farmed the land. Had a real spread at one time."

"Gee," Jody exclaimed, obviously impressed. "Your folks still own it?"

"Yes. My dad has been trying to sell off some of the land to help pay the taxes, but, since the Depression, nobody's buying anything."

More silence followed while Jody squirmed in the wet sand, obviously uncomfortable. Taffy looked at the dingy rag covering his injury.

"Tell us about St. Clair."

"A nice, quiet little village. Folks are friendly. They try to be helpful." A wistful look crossed Jeff's face. He absently reached out and picked up a white egret feather lying in the sea grass. He looked at it thoughtfully, turning it between his fingers, all traces of the bright, infectious smile gone.

"There's a man over there. Mr. Fulton. Owns a fish market. He couldn't put me to work, but he spent a lot of time talking about how some folks invent their own jobs."

"Invent their own jobs? How?"

"Well, like getting scallops and selling them, or cutting and drying sea oats. Sorting cup shells for sale. Things like that."

"Is that what you're doing?" Jody ventured innocently.

A sheepish half grin showed at the corners of Jeff's mouth. He looked away.

"What I've been doing is nothing but wasting time, Jamie. Spent one whole afternoon trying to shuck scallops at Mr. Fulton's place. It was like boring into concrete trying to get a knife into those pesky things. I never did get the hang of it. After three hours of mangling them and gouging my hands, I ended up with one pint."

Jeff looked into the two faces before him. "At first I was pleased with myself, thinkin' maybe I'd really done something worthwhile, until I remembered what Mr. Fulton told me. Thirty-five cents a quart. In my three hours of work, plus my time finding them, I had made a total of seventeen and a half cents."

Taffy heard a muffled snicker coming from Jody. She nudged him with her foot, discouraging him with a look. The city guy's plight had touched something inside her, bringing her to attention. All sorts of things were going through her mind. She wanted to hear more.

"What did you do with your scallops?"

"They were too hacked up to sell, so I ate them. The next day I got more and tried again, but by then my hands were so sore I made an even worse mess of it. Before the week was out, I knew I wasn't going to make any money with those things. I started working with cup shells instead."

"How did that work out?"

The last hint of wry amusement faded from Jeff's face, replaced by a look of total defeat. He shrugged his shoulders in a gesture of futility. "Might be all right for some, but I never seemed to make any headway at all. Been working at it day and night now for a week and ended up with two quarts. A dollar and fifty cents' worth."

Taffy stared at Jeff openly, her pulse quickening. In her eyes he was no longer the empty-headed, skulking intruder, aimlessly wiling away his time. He was a serious-minded young man from the city, hopelessly out of his element. He had little knowledge about the water and less about how to reap its harvest, but he had tried. All he needed was a little help.

She thought about the redfish she and Jody had caught that night by the old dock, the trout that fed on the grass flats, the mackerel and kings running through the pass.

"So that's why I'm leaving in the morning," Jeff went on. "I'll go back to Tampa and keep on looking for work. That's all I can do."

Another silence fell. Taffy stared at her feet.

"Where you kids from?" Jeff asked.

Taffy's head jerked up. She eyed Jeff skeptically. The miserable question that had to be asked had come out at last. There was no more time for evasion. She heard Jody groan, ever so softly, under his breath.

The question hung in the air. Jeff waited while the stony silence thickened, looking uncomfortable while he searched the faces before him. Finally, with a shrug of his shoulders, he turned aside. "You needn't tell me your business if you don't want to. I didn't come here to snoop, only to track down a whiff of smoke."

Jeff got up from his sitting position on the grass. The feather he had been holding fluttered to the ground. He studied the two youths long and searchingly before making his next comment. "Where you came from is not important, and I'm sorry if I've made you uncomfortable. But there's something that puzzles me." There was concern in his voice. "I'm not leaving here until I find out what this boy Jamie is doing here in his condition."

Jody came to life as though he had suddenly found himself sitting in a bed of ants. He rose to his knees, looking at Jeff with startled eyes. He began to speak but glanced at Taffy in time to read her warning look. In exasperation, he closed his mouth and slowly sank back in the wet sand.

"The boy is skin and bones, Chris. Doesn't look like he's had a square meal in six months. Besides, he's sick. Why is he here, camping on this deserted island, when he should be at home with his parents where he belongs? Where he could be taken care of?"

Taffy heard the concern in Jeff's voice. She was shrinking inside, her stomach already tied in knots, yet she met his eyes unwaveringly. "Jamie doesn't have any parents," she said simply.

Frustration deepened in Jeff's face. "Then who takes care of him?"

"Nobody. His parents are dead, and an uncle, who is supposed to take care of him, is an alcoholic. Jamie has been rooting for himself for a long time."

Jeff stared into Jody's flushed face, then turned back to Taffy, his voice considerably subdued. "And you, Chris? Surely your parents must have been aware of Jamie's condition before you two set out on this camping jaunt?"

"I don't have any parents either. My father died overseas in the war. I never knew him. My mother died of tuberculosis when I was three. I barely remember her. My grandfather, . . ." her voice faltered. Tears welled up in her eyes. "My grandfather took care of me all these years. He . . . he died recently."

Jeff groped for words. He shifted uneasily, looking from one to the other.

"Jamie isn't starving, Jeff. He's been slat thin all his life, but you're right about him being sick. He got a catfish fin stuck in his leg. He needs medicine. . . ." Her voice dropped away. "I figured on going someplace . . . to get some . . ."

"Chris, are you two kids in some kind of trouble?"

"Our trouble is Jamie's leg. He needs medicine. Peroxide. He was doing all right until he ran out of peroxide."

"Is it money you need?" Jeff asked quickly. "I'm flat broke, but maybe I can talk to Mr. Fulton . . ."

Taffy felt more tightening inside her. "No, we have money."

"I'll be glad to help any way I can, but there's something else I don't understand. Why haven't you gone after peroxide before now? Why have you put it off if you have the money to buy it?"

Just for an instant, a look of hardness came into the ice blue eyes that stared back at Jeff. When Taffy spoke, her voice was flat and toneless. "The law is looking for me."

Jody's body sagged into the wet sand while Jeff stared, openmouthed.

"Nobody's looking for Jamie—just me. I'm . . . I'm a runaway. I ran away from a welfare agent fixing to send me away after my grandfather died."

Jody suddenly roused himself from his slumped position to confront Jeff, his face the color of old ashes.

"Ain't no crime to run away," he bellowed. He raised himself to his knees and yelled louder. "You already heard her. She ain't got no parents, and no kin. So what's to run away from?"

Jody was fighting for control. His lower lip worked. Tears gathered in his eyes. In two long strides, Jeff was beside him, kneeling down in the edge of the water. He placed a firm hand on Jody's shoulder.

"Take it easy, fella. Nobody's going to run interference on either of you. Seems like the most important thing right now is to get you in shape." He looked up at Taffy. "In the morning, I'll row over to St. Clair and see if I can dig up some peroxide. If I don't find any there, I'll hitch a ride to Twin Oaks. I'll stick around here for a few days and see how Jamie gets along. If his leg isn't any better by then, I'll get him to a doctor."

Jody's eyes lit up as color rushed back in his face. *Jeff was going to help!* By this time tomorrow, or maybe even sooner, he would have peroxide again! He looked up at Jeff, a broad grin on his face.

Taffy searched for words, but nothing came out.

She looked up under the pines. Thin smoke from the stone hearth filtered upward. Steam rose from an iron pot.

She thought about the meager meals she had seen Jeff eating day after day. Skimpy portions of fish. Nothing else. Their own stock of food wasn't all that great any-

118

more either, but at least she and Jody had a few staples left—the kind that stuck to the ribs. She turned back to Jeff.

"We have a lot to talk about, Jeff. Why don't you have supper with us? We have a fair-sized pot of beans simmering over the coals. I'll fry up some flounder and make some hoecake. It'll be ready in about a half hour."

"Yeah!" Jody piped up. "We got a mess of blue crabs to boil, too."

Jeff's eyes brightened. A slow smile slid across his face. "You sure you have plenty?"

"We got more than we can eat," Jody announced with finality.

≈

Jody ate with more gusto than he had in days, first refilling Jeff's plate and then his own until most of the food was gone. Talk had been light and brisk during the meal, most of it being carried on by Jody and Jeff. Jeff politely avoided any further questions about Taffy's and Jody's past while Jody asked endless questions about Jeff's grandfather's way of life on the island. When the last plate was squared up, Taffy went to the hearth and brought back a steaming dish of bright red crabs, setting them down in the midst of the group to cool. Even Tar Baby, who had already had a meal of fish scraps and hoecake soaked in bean soppings, came to life to sniff the tantalizing aromas filling the air under the pines. Jody busied himself dissecting the crabs, carefully picking out the fatty chunks hidden in the lining for the cat. Taffy, who so far had contributed little to the conversation, turned her attention to Jeff.

"Been doing a lot of serious thinking, Jeff, about you not having much luck finding work."

"Yes?"

119

She cracked a crab claw with the handle of her knife, taking her time before going on. "That fish market over there in St. Clair. Where does your friend, Mr. Fulton, buy his seafood?"

"Mostly from fishermen in Ft. Myers. In large quantities. He has a big icehouse there for storage. Wholesales most of his stuff out in trucks to Tampa. His place is like a halfway house for distribution. The seafood he sells over the counter is only a sideline."

Jody, who had just stuffed his face with a handful of crabmeat, cut his eyes over at Taffy. He stopped chewing, looking at her intently. Taffy went on.

"Then if you was to go over there with a boatload of salable fish, he would buy them from you." It was more a statement than a question.

"Sure. Why do you ask?"

"It's like this," she responded quickly, her eyes bright with excitement. "Waters around here are teeming with fish. Mackerel and redfish running through the passes. Trout feeding on the grass flats. Groupers hanging around the rocks. Sheepsheads, flounder, mangrove snappers . . ."

A haggard look came into Jeff's eyes. He gestured in frustration. "That's fine for a seasoned fisherman with proper equipment, but I don't know anything about it."

Jody could contain himself no longer. "But we do, Jeff," he piped up in a loud voice. "Me and . . . er . . . Chris here. . . . Ain't no fish round here we don't know how to catch, and we got the tackle to do it, too! One night 'fore you got here we caught a whole mess of bull reds."

"That's right, Jeff," Taffy broke in. "That night, in less than two hours, we caught well over a hundred pounds of them. They would have sold for twice the money a laborer could make all day, but because we couldn't take them to market, we had to turn them loose."

Jeff sat spellbound. Before he could speak, Jody cut in

again. "But you could, Jeff! You could take 'em to St. Clair and sell 'em to that Mr. Fulton."

Taffy silenced him with a glance. Her eyes went back to Jeff. She spoke softly. "You see, Jeff, Jamie and I grew up in a fishing village. Fishin' comes as natural to us as breathin'. We can teach you. Make a real fisherman out of you in no time. You can make a decent wage right here on the island. Enough to eat on and send money home to your folks, too."

Jeff bounded to his feet. "You two—you really caught all that redfish? You're not putting me on?"

"No, we're not putting you on," she answered quietly, a slow smile touching her lips. "Would you like to have a go at the fish tomorrow night around sunset?"

"You can bet your life I would!"

≈ **20** ≈

The next morning at daybreak, Jeff shoved his rowboat from the dock and set out for St. Clair. He had four dollars of Jody and Taffy's money in his pocket, along with the list of medicine and groceries Taffy had given him. Finding no peroxide at the store in St. Clair, he hitched a ride to Twin Oaks, a small town twelve miles east on the Tamiami Trail. He bought three ounces of permanganate from Duffy's Drugs on Main Street, plus eight large bottles of peroxide. The cashier, a mousy little woman with streaks of gray in her hair, looked over his odd purchases but made no comment as she bagged them and rang up the sale.

Jeff headed back from St. Clair at ten o'clock. The medicines, along with the groceries, were stashed under the bow. Before he sat down to row, he looked at the green island in the distance where Jody and Taffy were waiting. Not Jamie Thomas or Chris Adams anymore, but Jody Hillard and Taffy Hansen, two ragtag wanderers from a fishing village far to the south.

As he rowed, a thought made him smile. He was remembering a strange feeling that had passed over him shortly after he had met the girl, Taffy, on the beach yesterday afternoon. He had seen a subtle grace in her movements, even under all those baggy clothes she was wearing, as well as a glint of irritation in her eyes that she had tried so hard to hide. He had not missed the rare

122

loveliness of the face hidden under that old hat, but when she took the hat off, revealing a lustrous crop of blond-white hair glowing in the sun, he knew he had found the answer to a mystifying experience he had had one night shortly after coming to the island.

He had been wading in shallow water in front of the house, the full moon overhead. It was so bright, he could see for miles around. Herons stood in the shallows where the ebb tide had drained the flats. Small ripples glistened over the surfaces of potholes, but there was a small, dark object in the distance that he couldn't make out. A mound of sea grass? A half-sunken log?

As he watched, he saw it move, or thought he did. It was too far away to be certain. Shortly afterward, he saw it rise like an apparition. He watched, mouth agape, while short hairs prickled at the back of his neck. He stared. The *thing* seemed to be drifting toward shore, dragging something. Finally, it disappeared in the shadow of the mangroves.

Jeff spent the rest of the evening pondering what he had seen. In the end, he concluded it had probably been a little old man because he had seen what appeared to be a head of white hair. But what would an old man be doing here? Foraging for something on the flats? Where had he stashed his boat?

The whole thing had been weird. Still, he had told himself, everything had an explanation.

Then, when he saw the girl's hair yesterday, he knew who he had seen that night. And when he saw the pile of clamshells onshore, he knew what she had been looking for.

Jeff laughed aloud. Now that it had all come into focus, he knew the vision he had seen was one he would never forget. The whole thing had impressed him so much that he found himself recalling all the girls he had ever known—the ones in grade school, in high school, his own sisters. He couldn't imagine even one of them out there on the flats alone in the moonlight, plodding over the slippery grass and soft mud in bare feet, digging clams.

But it wasn't only the girl who occupied Jeff's thoughts today. Ever since he got up this morning, he kept seeing the stained bandages coming off as Jody worked to loosen them. He saw the redness and the proud, angry flesh of the leg as more folds came off. And he saw the wound itself in all its stark ugliness. The boy's infection was out of control. Somewhere in the back of Jeff's mind the hateful word *gangrene* kept coming up.

He shoved the oars deeper in the water, wondering how he could possibly have allowed himself to be talked into going to town to buy peroxide. It was a doctor the boy needed!

When he rounded the tip end of Pelican Island, the offshore breeze died and the heat came down on him with a vengeance. He looked at the house dozing peacefully on pilings in the white sand and felt his pulse quicken. He was very attached to the little island his grandfather had homesteaded. More than anything else, he wanted to stay on, to learn how to harvest the waters, to become a part of that adventurous way of life.

He let his breath out slowly. Dared he hope those two in the lagoon could help him bring this about?

He pushed his thoughts to the back of his mind, concentrating instead on finding the hopelessly camouflaged opening to the lagoon—the place he had passed by so often without knowing of its existence.

When he turned his head to judge the distance he had come, he saw a skiff in the edge of the mangroves. Taffy stood in the stern, waiting. A hat covered her face.

He smiled. She had known all along he wouldn't find that opening.

≈ **21** ≈

The following morning, Jeff pulled in at Mr. Fulton's boat dock at dawn, determined to be on hand as soon as the fish market owner appeared.

He shoved the bow of his boat to shore and eased overboard in ankle-deep water to throw out the anchor. He was glad enough to get out of the boat. Because of the heavy load he was carrying, it had messed up all the way from Pelican Island and been nearly impossible to keep on a steady course.

He straightened up, flexing his muscles. A film of dried fish slime covered the front of his dungarees. Scales clung to his shirt.

He walked out on the dock and sat down, looking admiringly at the pile of fish in the boat. The early sun touched the moist scales of the bull reds, bringing out hues of gray and pink, with amber around the throats and black spots at the tails.

He had been looking at these fish ever since he set out this morning, but he still felt a flush of excitement as he relived the magic of the night before. He had stood in the edge of the dark water and thrown out his handline with its strange collection of swivels and sinkers. He had waited expectantly—for what, he wasn't sure—while the wash of water played at his ankles and the stars cast their soft glow around him. Light from the fire on the beach had flickered over Jody's shirt where he sat in the water, slowly paying out his line as the currents nudged it into deeper water. Then, all at once, Jeff had felt the electrifying jolt of his own line, momentarily throwing him off balance while his heart raced. Jody had shouted, "Get him to shore, Jeff!"

Hand over hand, he had pulled the fish in—the biggest, most beautiful redfish anyone could ever hope to catch. He had wanted to take the fish to the firelight to examine and admire it, but Jody kept nagging away. "Come on, Jeff! Bait up and throw out again. We have to get 'em while they're hittin'."

Like someone in a trance, he had turned away from his fish and reached into the bucket for a ghost crab, forgetting for the moment about the small claws and the eight sharp-tipped legs. In his excitement, the crab's sharp pinch had gone unnoticed. By the time he had thrown out his line again, Jody was struggling with his own line. Then Taffy had appeared from the shadows, breathless and flushed, with more ghost crabs clutched tight in her hands.

And that was the way the evening had gone, Jeff reflected. Taffy had tracked down the bait while he and Jody had pulled in redfish until Jody, winded, had turned his line over to Taffy.

Long after Jeff had retired for the night, he'd tossed and turned, reliving those magic moments. Twice during the night he had gotten out of bed and walked down to the boat to marvel at the magnificent pile of fish heaped up in the stern.

Jeff smiled. The lure of fishing was already in his blood!

Mr. Fulton beamed as he adjusted the weights of his scale. Jeff put the wire fish basket, overflowing with bull reds, on the platform.

"Figgered all along you'd hit onto something sooner or later, son. I have to give you credit. This is a nice mess of fish you brought in." He chuckled. "Guess this will keep you in grub for a while." He straightened up to look at Jeff. "Going to have a go at it again tonight?"

"Yes, sir. With luck, maybe I'll be bringing in some more tomorrow morning."

Jeff fingered the receipt Mr. Fulton handed him. One hundred and sixty pounds of bottom fish at two and a half cents a pound—four dollars' worth! He caught his breath.

"Thank you, sir," he said, smiling broadly as he stuffed the receipt in his pocket. Everything was taking on new meaning, and Jeff felt a deep sense of gratitude for those two back in the lagoon. Jody, with his expert knowledge of fishing, his eagerness and patience when he explained each detail of his work to Jeff while he rigged the outfits and talked about the habits of the fish. And the bewitching young lady, Taffy. Her words kept coming back to him, the words she had spoken that first day in the lagoon: "Make a real fisherman out of you in no time. You can make a decent wage right here. . . ."

When he left the fish house for his boat, the sun had set the water aflame. To Jeff, a morning had never looked more beautiful, nor held more promise.

≈

While Jeff was in St. Clair with the load of fish, Taffy and Jody, back at the lagoon, ate their breakfast of oatmeal laced sparingly with syrup and canned cream. A pot of clam chowder, thick with potatoes and rice, simmered over the coals. Jeff would be hungry when he got back.

"Been thinkin' something, Miss Taffy," Jody spoke up. "Seen a man once on the beach at Boca Grande Pass. He was shoveling fine shell into croaker sacks to take home to his wife and kids to wash down and sieve out for sortin'. Said what he was workin' with wasn't just any

127

old shell—that what he hauled home had plenty of cup shells mixed in with it."

"What about it, Jody?"

"Well, that man said with everybody pitchin' in like that, they picked up some extra money."

"Well," Taffy countered skeptically, "Jeff couldn't do anything with his, and he worked at it day and night."

"Just got me a hunch Jeff was workin' with poor shell. That man said he had to hunt around for the best kind, and I think I know where some of it is."

Taffy glanced up at Jody with interest. "Where's that?"

"Down at the south pass where them mangroves grow right on the beach. Fine shell is piled up around the roots there three feet deep in some places."

Taffy didn't answer.

"Been thinkin' like this, Miss Taffy. There's things round here I can't do until my leg gets better, and instead of just hangin' around sometimes, I could be foolin' with them shells. Maybe Jeff could go down there in his boat sometime and haul some of that stuff back. I could sieve it out in the water and start sortin' when it's dry."

He put his spoon down and looked at Taffy thoughtfully. "I'd like that, Miss Taffy."

Taffy's interest had picked up considerably. She fiddled with her spoon while she mulled over Jody's proposition. If there *was* a good source of shell down at the south pass, maybe they could all have a hand in it, like on Sunday, when they couldn't fish because the fish house was closed, or after supper when the work was finished.

"Tell you what, Jody. Soon as I get squared away here, I'll hike down there and look around."

"Gee, Miss Taffy, that will be great, 'cept it's a long way. Four miles at least."

"I'll be down in no time," she said, getting to her feet. "In the meantime, you can tell me more about what I'm going to be looking for."

On the way to the pass, Taffy came across a fresh turtle crawl where a big loggerhead had come ashore to lay eggs. Deep tracks from the water's edge to the base of the bluff plainly showed where the turtle had lumbered through the sand. Dried sea grass and patches of uprooted sea oats marked the site of the nest.

Excitement went through her. She dropped to her knees, carefully digging into the lightly packed sand, her fingers working in anticipation. Wouldn't Jody be pleased to stuff his mouth with some of these!

Then, all at once, her fingers became still. A thoughtful look crossed her face. She was in another place, another time, her grandfather beside her on his knees as they both dug into turtle nests. The same excitement had gone through her then as she'd listened to her grandfather's gentle voice: "We won't be digging too deep, lass. Some of these little fellers has to be left behind to hatch out and go their way."

She drew her hands back slowly, her body coming to rest on the backs of her heels. She thought about her grandfather's words and the turtle that had crawled up to this place in the dead of night. Apprehensive about being on land, yet not hurrying with her task. A two-hour process ahead of her, to be dispensed in thoroughness and order, dropping the eggs slowly and methodically until her organs had been emptied out. No eggs broken. None misplaced.

Taffy let her breath out in a sigh. Leaning forward, she scraped at the sand again until her fingertips made contact with the first egg, about the size of a Ping-Pong ball. She picked it up carefully, feeling the strange pliability of the shell molding to her touch. She put it back in the nest and covered it up.

On the way back, she would fill her hat with some of those good fresh eggs, she told herself as she hiked on down the beach. Maybe two or three dozen, or whatever she could carry easily. That wouldn't be robbing the nest. After all, there were a hundred or more down there. Her grandfather would approve of that.

The pass at the south end was unlike the one that flowed peacefully past the cypress house. This one was narrow and treacherous. Even before she reached it, she could see turbulent currents swirling around the shoals, spewing spray and foam in the air. Rocks jutted out from shore, forming small tide pools on the beach. Low-growing mangroves cropped out, stopping just inside the high-tide mark. And, piled deep around the tangle of red prop roots, were the mounds of shell Jody had described. She sank to her knees, digging into the moist, bleached mound. She dug until her hands reached the core of the mound as Jody had instructed. She scooped up a handful of the fine shell, examining it closely, and saw the unmistakable concentration of round, snow white cup shells Jody had talked about. She dug deeper, using both hands, staring in fascination at the tiny shells, the very smallest of the clam family. Jody had been right! There were millions of those little cup shells buried deep in the warm center of the mound.

She stuffed her shirt pockets with the mixture and headed back, thinking of the possibilities that lay ahead. Like the man said, if they all pitched in, there was extra money to be made. Jody would be delighted with her findings.

≈ 22 ≈

Now that they were certain of a ready market in St. Clair, the three ambitious beachcombers stepped up their activities considerably. Besides the catch of redfish each night, Jody was bringing in sheepsheads and flounder from the lagoon during the day. Taffy, equipped with calcutta poles and live bait, taught Jeff to fish the grass beds for trout. She also taught him to pole a skiff.

What was the big deal with poling a skiff? Jeff wanted to know. What was wrong with his own boat?

"Your rowboat isn't designed for hauling heavy loads. It's too cumbersome. Poling a slender skiff is a lot easier than straining at a pair of oars."

Shoving the skiff around was easy, Jeff discovered, but keeping it headed in the right direction was something else, especially when he found himself in the middle of the sound in a brisk offshore breeze. Once he got the hang of it, however, his interest began to pick up. She showed him how to "walk the oar," beginning at the bow end of the boat and shoving hard on the pole while making long strides to the stern, then back to the bow to repeat the operation all over again. With unexpected speed, the little craft shot over the water.

Taffy showed Jeff how to use the pole in deep water, how to buck the wind and tide to best advantage and with the least effort. By the time the lessons were finished, Jeff was pleased with himself and genuinely impressed by the performance of the boat.

Because it was important to get the fish to market in good condition, sometimes Jeff had to make two trips a day to St. Clair, but he didn't care. The first time he went in with a load of trout, however, he was due for a surprise. He was thinking about the two and a half cents per pound for bottom fish when Mr. Fulton happily handed him a receipt for fifty-two pounds of trout at *seven cents a pound.* Jeff was speechless. Three dollars and sixty-four cents more to add to the growing collection of receipts!

From the beginning, the three of them had agreed to set aside a given amount of their earnings for groceries and other common necessities. The rest they would divide equally. Jody and Taffy decided they wouldn't spend any of their money. They wanted to watch it grow each week. But Jeff had plans for his, plans he knew would require careful handling. First, he would send money home each week to his mother. Already he could see himself at the post office purchasing the money order, and the flush of pride and pleasure he knew would come to his mother's face when she saw the green certificate.

After that, he would set money aside for the other thing he had been considering since the night of the big redfish catch: the house. If he was going to stay there, he had to make it livable. As it was, he couldn't sleep there without burning a smudge pot all night. Replacing the screens would come first, and screen wire cost money. He would have to go slow.

One day, he talked to Mr. Fulton about it. The older man thought a moment before offering a comment. "Tell you what, son. Give me a list of what you need for the screens, and I'll pick up the stuff for you. You don't have to order piecemeal. I'll buy enough for you to do the whole house, and you can pay me a little on it each week."

Jeff was delighted. As soon as he had an opportunity, he rummaged through the old lumber pile in back of the house and sorted out pieces he could use to patch weather cracks and reinforce window casings. He took out rotted screens and patched others that were still serviceable, all the while making a list: paint for the windowsills, new wicks for the kerosene stove, hinges for the sagging doors, nails. On and on. If he was going to do it at all, he reminded himself, he may as well do it right.

≈ **23** ≈

Mr. Fulton's eyes sparkled when he tallied up Jeff's fish at the end of the first week and handed the receipt to him. All told, Jeff had brought in eight hundred pounds of bottom fish and one hundred and five pounds of trout, making a total of twenty-seven dollars and thirty-five cents.

"Guess I already told you, Jeff, you're the only one around doing any fishing in these waters. Folks here are all farmers. A few men south of here do some offshore fishing—grouper and red snapper mostly—but other than that, I have to depend on everything coming up from Ft. Myers. You sure fired up my interest, son. You're doing a great job."

"Thank you, sir," Jeff answered slowly, feeling uncomfortable about the undeserved praise. He couldn't wait to see the faces of his two friends when they divided up the money. Besides that, his stomach was beginning to growl. He wondered what Taffy was cooking.

He was thinking about Taffy a lot lately. He found himself looking often into her wistful face to make sure that everything was all right with her, and that he was measuring up in her eyes. He wasn't quite sure why this was so, except that something had happened to him the very first time he set eyes on her. Underneath all that animosity showing in her face, he was sure he had detected something more—something that had made him to want to protect her in some way.

Jeff felt sure now that what he had seen had to do with the recent loss of her grandfather. If so, he wanted her to know that she could count on him to help make things better. He had seen her anxious about Jody, and for that reason he had become as solicitous as she, sharing the burden, watching over the boy as if he were his brother. Daily, he applied the peroxide and rubbed aloe, which they'd found growing on the island, into Jody's tender pink skin. There was little change, at least none Jeff could see, but the boy was holding his own. The wound looked clean enough, and Jody was eating everything in sight. He surely looked better than when Jeff had found him sleeping in the wet sand that first day in the lagoon.

As Jeff poled back to the island, he looked at the rolls of screen in the boat. When the old house was fixed up, he reminded himself, he could offer his home to Taffy and the boy. Surely that would help ease some of their discomforts.

When he got to the lagoon, Jody was boiling crabs in a pot over the coals. Taffy stirred lima beans over another hearth, and nearby, on a piece of canvas spread under the pines, was a dish of ripe tomatoes and a pie pan of cooked turtle eggs. Jeff warmed to the cheerful scene.

"Did you get the money, Jeff? Can we count it now?"

Jody's exuberance was contagious. Taffy's eyes brightened. She gave the beans one more stir and carried the pot over to the canvas spread. They all sat in a circle. Jeff dug in his pockets for the money and receipts. Because Mr. Fulton had paid him in one-dollar bills, the pile looked impressive.

"I paid for the tackle," Jeff explained, handing the receipt to Taffy. "And I took out three dollars for myself. It was for some money I owed Mr. Fulton."

Jeff counted out three dollars and gave it to Taffy, then

three more for Jody. He gave the other receipts to Taffy, who was bookkeeper for the group. The rest of the money was split three ways.

"Boy! This is somethin'," Jody squealed, stuffing his money in a jar. Taffy fingered hers thoughtfully, smiling to herself. Jeff stared down at his share of bills. He picked them up, one by one, and slipped them in his pocket. Monday morning, he could send the money order. There would be money left over to pay for more repairs on the house. And the grocery money for the coming week had already been set aside!

He let his breath out slowly. How could his world have changed so drastically in one short week? He was actually making money—and good money at that—besides learning a useful trade he could draw on for the rest of his life. How could he ask for more?

"Maybe next week we can catch even more fish, Jeff. . . ."

"Been thinking about that, Jody," Jeff answered. "But we can't be pushing too far. Mr. Fulton already thinks I'm some kind of a genius, bringing in all that fish this week. After all, we don't want him to start wondering."

"Jeff's right, Jody," Taffy said.

Jody nodded. He spooned beans into his mouth with one hand and reached for the crabs with the other. He looked up at Jeff. "What did you owe Mr. Fulton three dollars for?"

"Jody!" Taffy chided. "That's none of your business."

"It's all right," Jeff said easily. "I was going to tell you anyway."

He explained about how he wanted to fix up the house to make it livable, and Mr. Fulton's part in it. "The three dollars was my first payment on it."

Before Jody or Taffy had a chance to comment, Jeff went on. "I'd be right proud to share my house with you two when I'm finished with it."

136

Jody started to speak, then hesitated, looking over at Taffy. She had set her plate down and was staring at Jeff. *Fix the old house up! Make it livable!* Jeff was planning to stay on the island. He would go on hauling fish to market. Her future and Jody's were secure!

Jeff went on. "There's plenty of room, and we'd all be more comfortable. I'll first screen the windows, then make a screen door and hang it at the main entrance for more ventilation. I'll patch the porch roof and fix the steps and get the kerosene stove working. . . ."

Taffy sat very still, visualizing the old cypress house breathing with new life under Jeff's touch, bursting with light inside. Lamplight streaming through the open windows in the evening, cheefulness flooding away the gloom. Was that wonderful old place finally going to regain the grace and respectability it was entitled to?

Taffy was seeing other things, too. After countless meals cooked over campfires, and pots she could never get clean, thinking about the kerosene stove, a dishpan of warm sudsy water on the counter, the pump just outside the back door seemed like sheer luxury. She had almost forgotten what it was like to sit in a chair, to eat a meal at a table, to sleep in a bed.

The temptation to move into the house was strong. Still, there were things to consider. She remembered her wariness about the place when they'd first come to the island, how she had hidden the boats under the dock, and the sense of being watched.

Was she being unreasonable now? she asked herself. Finally she spoke up. "What about your folks, Jeff? Won't they be coming here once in a while for a vacation, or to see how you're doing?"

"Thought about that, Taffy, but I doubt it. It's almost impossible for them to get away. My dad puts in long hours working two jobs. Besides, he wouldn't leave with-

137

out my mom, and she can't tolerate the mosquitoes here."

Jeff thought a moment before going on. "Mr. Fulton has a truck going to Tampa once or twice a week. Said I could go with him when I wanted to. When I get squared away here, I'll go and see them. Long as they know I'm all right, they won't be coming here."

Jody was taking it all in. He glanced over at Taffy. Her eyes were glowing, and he could see two red spots coloring her cheeks. He couldn't stand the suspense any longer.

"Come on, Miss Taffy. You heard what Jeff said. Have you forgotten we're a hundred miles from home? What are you waitin' for?"

Taffy ignored him. She looked up at Jeff.

"I . . . I don't know how to say this, Jeff. It all sounds so . . . tantalizing. If you're sure it's all right. I've had a special feeling about that house . . . about seeing it fixed up. . . ."

Her words, once loosened up, now tumbled out. "I stood in that big room one day, the one with all those casement windows, and closed my eyes and visualized how it would look all cleaned up, glass sparkling in the sun, bright-colored curtains fluttering in the breeze, throw rugs on the floor, and wildflowers in a vase on the table. And Jeff, . . ." she went on, "if we're going to be living up there, too, we're going to pay our share of the expenses."

She fished in her pocket and promptly produced her three dollars.

"Yeah, Jeff," Jody shouted, unscrewing the lid to his money jar.

"I'm going to help you, too," Taffy said. "I'll scrub the walls and floors and wash the windows and dust the shelves and clean up the yard and . . . when can we get started?"

Jeff fingered the bills in his hands, protesting that he didn't expect or want their money, but neither of them would hear of his refusal.

Jody, in the meantime, had worked up his own speech. "I'm going to help, too," he piped, looking into Taffy's face. "I can sharpen tools and hammer out old bent nails, and maybe get started on that bag of shell Jeff brought up from the south pass. That old round table would be just the place to work on cup shells."

≈ 24 ≈

Jody, seated in one of the captain's chairs, nibbled on an orange while he sorted cup shells from the pile in the center of the big round table. Using a sea gull feather to help him, he flipped deftly at the handful spread out before him, shoving the trash shell to one side and sliding the delicate cup shells into a wooden bowl. His leg soaked in a steaming pail of permanganate water.

Steady pounding sounds came through the windows from outside where Jeff worked. By sundown, Jeff would be finished. The whole house would be screened, and tonight he and Miss Taffy would not be sleeping in the lean-to. They would sleep in real beds, each in a bedroom all their own, with no pesky mosquitoes to chew on them. Jeff had even brushed kerosene into the screen mesh, so there weren't going to be any sand flies biting into his scalp when the breeze died down, either.

Jody was like a child at Christmas with his mind jumping from one new thing to another. Each of them in a bedroom of their own! That was something Jody had never had in his life. Nor a dresser, for that matter.

Tonight, Miss Taffy would cook supper on the stove in the kitchen, and later she was going to make him some chocolate fudge to nibble on when he soaked his leg again. But what he looked forward to most was the knowledge that the evening meals would be shared in a clean, cheerful room in a real home. They were like a family now, Jody reflected. *His* family. Jeff and Miss Taffy smiling at him from across the table in the soft light of the lamp. To Jody, it was paradise.

Taffy came out of one of the bedrooms lugging a mop and pail of sudsy water in one hand, a broom and dustpan in the other. Her face was flushed with perspiration, but there was a glow of satisfaction in her eyes. She had been cleaning the inside of the house all day. A scent of yellow soap followed her into the room. She set the mop and pail down and went over to him. "How's it going, Jody?"

He picked up the wooden bowl and poured his cup shells into a clean quart jar. He held it up to her. It was almost half full. Taffy's eyes lit up.

"Gosh, Jody. If we all worked on them like that. . . . Never thought about using a feather. Won't Jeff be surprised!"

Jody warmed to Taffy's enthusiasm. "Maybe after supper I can sort some more."

"Maybe we all can, Jody," she said thoughtfully, glancing around the spacious room. "This is the only room I haven't cleaned yet. Then I'll be through, except for getting supper started."

"Anything you want me to do?"

"Well, . . . you could sand the rust off the stove grates for me. That would be a big help."

"Sure, Miss Taffy."

Taffy moved the pail of permanganate water out onto the front porch. She seated Jody at a bench with a piece of sandpaper and two very rusty grates, picked up her broom and dustpan, and went back in.

Jody watched her work out of the corner of his eye as he ground away at the grates. He noticed that she was cleaning every part of the room except where the fireplace stood. It was almost as though she was saving that for last.

Finally, when everything else was finished except

scrubbing the floor, he saw her move to the far wall. She washed down the massive travertine structure and polished the mantel. She swept out the hearth, then stood for a while staring up at the painting on the wall. She pulled up a chair, stood on it, and gently, almost reverently, lifted the frame from the wall. A dark patch showed in the woodwork where the painting had been. She stepped down, wiping cobwebs from the corners with her fingers. Then she went over to a window and called to Jeff to come inside.

He stepped carefully around the furniture Taffy had placed in the middle of the room and looked at her questioningly.

"This painting, Jeff. It's a hundred years old—a John Audubon original. Tell us what you know about it."

Jeff wiped dirt from his hands as he looked at it thoughtfully. "It belonged to my grandfather. He brought it out here when the house was first built. But I don't know how it came to be left here. An oversight, I suspect."

"How did your grandfather come by it? Did he buy it?"

"No, it was given to one of my ancestors by the great artist himself."

Taffy stared at Jeff in awe. "You're not serious," she breathed out in a whisper.

Jeff smiled at her. "It's quite a story."

At this point, Jody took his foot out of the pail and went inside to hear what Jeff had to say.

Back in the early 1800s, Jeff told them, when the government was still trying to rid the Florida Keys of piracy and Indian uprisings, some of Jeff's people lived on Indian Key. They made their living from the waters, and it was there one of Jeff's great-great-uncles befriended John Audubon, the man already noted for his paintings of American birds.

This uncle was handy with small craft. He could ease

around the islands in Florida Bay in stealth and silence, barely making a ripple as his boat slipped over the shallow waters. Mr. Audubon hired him to help seek out a rare and exotic water bird that had completely captivated his interest. It was the white heron shown in the painting, Jeff explained. The bird was a native of South America and, until that spring in 1832, had never been sighted on North American soil.

The great artist became obsessed with the grace and beauty of the four-foot-tall, snow white creature that sailed around the green mangroves and stalked the blue waters in search of food. He stopped at nothing to learn all he could about his special find. He and Jeff's great-great uncle set out each morning at dawn, often not returning until after dark. Mr. Audubon traveled the waterways day after day, his skin burning in the sun, plagued by mosquitoes, sometimes standing in water up to his hips while he painted the magnificent bird. He had come to think of it as something to be revered, a bird so special that he named it Angel of the Swamp.

Jeff paused in his story, and no one moved or spoke. Jody sat spellbound in the captain's chair while Taffy stood speechless, caught up in Mr. Audubon's romantic encounters with his white heron.

"Before Mr. Audubon left the island," Jeff went on, "he presented my uncle with this painting. The gift was a token of his appreciation of my uncle's loyalty and patience during the long, hot months on the waters of Florida Bay."

"So, this is his angel," Taffy said softly, running her fingers over the smooth inscriptions at the bottom of the painting. "I can't describe how I feel about this painting. . . ." She looked up at Jeff. "We can keep it here, can't we? You won't take it back to Tampa?"

Jeff beamed. "Of course we'll keep it here."

Jody wanted to get a closer look at the painting Miss

Taffy was so hopped up about. What could be so special about a painting of an old bird standing in the water next to a bunch of mangroves—even if it *was* by a famous artist? But as he stood at Miss Taffy's elbow, he, too, became enchanted. "Don't know why somebody didn't come along and swipe it," he said after a while.

"Because," Taffy stated matter-of-factly. "It was covered up with dust and cobwebs. Nobody could see its beauty—or Mr. Audubon's name at the bottom."

≈ **25** ≈

It was almost daylight when Jody slipped out of the lagoon and headed back to the house. He pulled hard at the oars of Jeff's rowboat, wanting to get back as quickly as possible. His prized collection of bottles, snugly wrapped in rags and stuffed in a canvas bag, lay on the stern seat.

It had been a week now since they had moved into the house. Because of all the activity, he had had no time to get back to his bottles still on the dune in the lagoon. And then, when the opportunity to go had presented itself, he couldn't figure out a way to get there. He knew Miss Taffy wouldn't like it if he poled his skiff. It would be too much of a strain on his leg. So he had to figure out some other way to get there without Jeff or Taffy knowing.

Rowing Jeff's boat had been the answer. By rowing, he wouldn't have to stand on his bum leg. Once the idea had come to him, he had itched for the opportunity to slip away. The prospect of seeing Miss Taffy's face when she saw his elegant display gleaming in the niches of the fireplace even now sent tingling sensations up and down his spine. He pulled harder on the oars.

But there was no reason to hurry. Jeff and Miss Taffy were out in the sound fishing for trout. It would be hours before they would come in.

Jody eased up on the oars. He was getting a little

winded. The steep climb up the dune where he had stashed his bottles had started the dull ache in his leg again, even though he had soaked it earlier while Miss Taffy was fixing breakfast by lamplight.

Despite his excitement, he couldn't help feeling the nagging depression that plagued him so often. Was his leg *never* going to heal? How he wished he could go fishing with Jeff and Miss Taffy instead of sitting onshore day after day.

After he had started using the peroxide again, Jody felt sure it would get his leg to show signs of improvement. Yet it had not. The ugly pus was still in his bandages each morning when he woke up, and when he exercised in the water, his leg got to throbbing so bad he had to crawl back home. For that reason, Jeff had made him a crutch, using a forked limb from a cedar tree. He had trimmed it to size and sanded down the rough edges. After that, Jody had been able to get around more easily.

It was true, Jody reminded himself, his leg was not getting any worse. But it wasn't getting any better, either.

He shrugged. What was he complaining about? After all, a lot of other things *had* improved. Three weeks ago, he couldn't have begun to do what he was doing now. He simply hadn't had the strength. This morning, there had been no feeling of strain, no dizziness or weakness. And when he had finished putting his bottles in place, he could soak his leg again. The pain would ease up. So why should he feel depressed? When his leg was good and ready, it would force out the last bits of broken catfish fin and the festering would stop. Then, and only then, would it begin to heal. Jody just wished it would happen soon.

Tar Baby was on the beach waiting for him. Jody tied the rowboat where Jeff had left it and carefully picked up his bag of bottles. "Come on Tar, let's go home. I got work to do."

The cat swished around Jody's legs for a moment before trotting on ahead. Jody lugged his load awkwardly over the soft sand. The fragile glass fish bottle with the fins and spines was safely tucked inside his shirt.

Once a pail of permanganate water was heating on the stove, Jody began washing the sand off the pieces in his bag. He dried them carefully and wiped away the fingerprints so that each bottle sparkled. He removed the broken pink murex from the fireplace, replacing it with the bright blue hip flask shaped like a clam. He chose a place for the smoke gray decanter with the glass stopper. He took his time, arranging and rearranging to place the colored glass in the best possible way. The sea greens and blues showed up best against the white background of the stonework. He tucked the ambers in against pale gray stones, and the green perfume bottle in a small place beside the white bits of coral. The lavender fish bottle went on top of the mantel.

When he stepped back to survey his work, a smile of genuine pleasure lit his face. The fireplace had always been a handsome piece of work, but the brilliant colors of the glass brought out a new beauty. "Boy, what a display!"

Jody finally settled down at the table, his leg in the pail of hot water. He picked up his feather and began work on the cup shells while he waited for Jeff and Miss Taffy to come home.

≈

By the time Jeff and Taffy got back, Jody had another half pint of cup shells to add to the growing collection of filled jars on the mantel.

Jody knew that Jeff would be the first to come into the

147

house to pick up his thermos of coffee before going on to St. Clair with the fish. When he heard the footsteps on the front porch, he felt a tingle of excitement. Jeff walked into the room, then stopped short when he saw the unexpected color gleaming in the niches of the fireplace. He stared in awe at the bottles as he picked them up, one by one, turning them over in his hands. He saw the splendor of the intricate fish bottle on the mantel. He reached out to touch it, then drew his hand back. He turned to Jody. "They're fantastic! Where did they come from?"

Jody squirmed with delight. He told Jeff about how each piece had come into his possession, and about the process he had used to bring out the colors.

"Gosh, Jody, if we can find more glass to color, I'll bet Mr. Fulton, with his connections in St. Petersburg, could sell it for us. Tourists would love this, especially if they know it's colored with that combination of Florida sun and white beach sand."

Jody was beside himself. He hadn't even thought about that!

Then Taffy came in. She, too, saw the colorful display. "Where on earth did they come from?"

Jody didn't answer. Taffy examined the sea green perfume bottle and turned to face him. He was grinning.

"Jody!" she exclaimed. "This isn't. . . . It can't be. . . . Is it?"

"Isn't what, Miss Taffy?" Jody asked, knowing full well what she meant.

"Those old bottles . . . you carried around in your boat?"

"The same ones, Miss Taffy." Jody gloated. "The same ones you found in my gear in Cranes Bog."

"But what . . . what did you *do* to them? They were just a bunch of old bottles when I saw them."

Jody explained all over again.

"Where did you get the idea? I mean, about puttin' 'em out in the sun?"

"Mr. Garvin told me about it a long time ago. Once, before the Depression, he packed his wife and kids in his car and made a trip out west. Someplace in Arizona, his wife went in a gift shop that had a lot of colored glass displayed in the window. 'Desert Glass' they called it. They had all kinds of fancy wine goblets, expensive ashtrays, cut-glass candy dishes and finger bowls—things like that—that some lady out there colored with the hot desert sun and dry sand. After Mr. Garvin told me that, I got to thinkin' I'd like to try doing the same thing here. I didn't have much to work with, at least none of the fancy things Mr. Garvin had described, so that's when I started scroungin' around for odd-shaped bottles."

"Looks like I better be doing the same thing, Jody. I'd sure like to see how this hobby of yours works," Jeff said. He picked up his thermos and headed for the door. "From now on, I'll keep my eyes open."

"Do that, Jeff," Taffy said, fingering the lavender fish bottle on the mantel. "Find me one like this."

≈ **26** ≈

Jody was in waist-deep water shucking scallops beside the floating trap when Jeff, bare to the waist and wearing cut-off dungarees, came poling up in one of the skiffs. He had just returned from the south pass with a load of shell.

"I got everything here for you, Jeff. Are you ready to start working on some scallops?"

"Put it this way, Jody," Jeff answered with a grin. "I'm as ready as I'll ever be, soon as I unload the shell on the dock."

"I already got some shucked out. Miss Taffy says we're going to have 'em for supper. She's going to coat 'em in flour and fry 'em in that big iron skillet."

"Sounds great. Hope we have plenty. I'm starved already."

Jody held up a pint jar he had set inside the trap to keep out of the sun. It was full.

"There's that many more in the trap still to be opened."

"Gosh, they look good! You're really something, Jody. How long did it take you to do that?"

"Dunno, didn't time myself. But it didn't take long."

Jeff finished with his boat and waded over to Jody. He peered inside the trap. Rays of filtered light reflected off the white sand below. The scallops rested peacefully, one on top of the other, with mouths slightly open.

Hundreds of bright blue eyes looked up at him from every corner of the trap.

He picked one up. The little round mollusk lay docile in his hand, making no move to tighten up. Jeff eased it back into the trap.

"I want to see you operate before I start in on my own, Jody. To begin with, go on like I wasn't here watching, like maybe you wanted to get the job done in a hurry. I'll tell you when to slow down."

Jody knew that Jeff had never seen a seasoned shucker open a scallop before. Jeff probably wanted to satisfy himself that it could be done as fast and as easily as he and Miss Taffy had described. All right, Jeff, Jody thought, grinning inwardly, I'll give you my best shot.

With that, he dipped his hand in and brought out a scallop. It was already positioned in his palm. With two easy strokes of his paring knife, he cut the muscle free from each shell and dropped it in a pan resting on the trap. At the same time, he reached in and brought out another scallop. He worked steadily and with ease, making no clumsy or wasted movements. At first, he took his time, but then he picked up speed until at last it seemed as though shells were hitting the water at the same time that white muscles hit the pan, almost like raindrops from the sky. Jeff stared in fascination.

"Uh, Jody, you can stop now. I get the message. Good gosh, I never expected to see anything quite like that. How long you been doing that?"

Jody's dark eyes danced. He was right in his element. "Since I was a little kid. I used to shuck scallops for Mr. Tanner back in our village. Mostly I'd bring 'em in to him already shucked, but other times some of the village matrons would get together and go out with all their younguns, dogs, cousins, aunts, and grandmothers and bring in washtubs full of scallops. They'd sell 'em unshucked. Then Mr. Tanner would hunt up the best

151

shuckers in the village, and we would all sit out there in his fish house, sometimes till midnight, workin' on 'em. You learn fast when you're gettin' paid for it."

"I'll bet you was the fastest one in the bunch, Jody."

"Not really. We all worked about the same, but I'll say this—he never left me out. I was always called on, and our group all got paid the same."

"Do you think I can ever learn to do that like you do?"

"Sure you can, but not in one day. You have to keep at it to shuck like I was doing."

"Well, I'm ready to start learning, but first I have to get something to put the shells in. Mr. Fulton has a use for them."

"Huh? What use?"

"I'll tell you and Taffy about it at supper."

"OK, but there's already a bunch of 'em down here in the water. See those little fish feasting on the guts? When we're through here, it will be a good time to catch bait for your fishing tomorrow."

"Good idea!"

Jeff came back with a foot tub and set it on top of the trap. He was ready to begin the lesson. This time, Jody opened his scallops with slow, deliberate movements. He took his time, explaining each step as he went along. It looked simple enough to Jeff: There was no prying or digging with the knife as Jeff had once experienced.

With a hollow feeling in his stomach, Jeff picked up a paring knife and slipped the blade inside the scallop he held in his hand. He cut the top shell loose as Jody had instructed. He inspected the bottom half still in his hand. A mass of strange little organs in various shapes and colors lay in a cluster in the shell, the top of the white muscle showing at the center. All he had to do now was slip the knife blade down beside it and cut once more. When he tried, however, he found that the stroke, performed so easily by the expert beside him, wasn't nearly as simple as it had seemed. Each time he tried it, he cut the muscle loose with no trouble, but the slippery entrails clung tight around it, refusing to come off without a hassle.

Jody came to his rescue. "Getting the muscle untangled from the guts can be tricky. Let's try another way to get you going."

He cut another top shell away, leaving the muscle stuck to the bottom shell. Using the point of his knife and his fingers, he lifted the guts out of the shell in one easy operation and dropped them in the water, leaving the bare muscle resting in the shell. The rest was easy.

Jeff was delighted. For the first time in his life, he was actually opening scallops without working himself into a frenzy. It wasn't important that Jody was shucking two to his one. Jeff would catch up soon enough; for now he was getting the job done. He felt a sense of accomplishment as he dropped perfectly shaped muscles into the pan beside Jody's.

When there were no more scallops to open, Jody slipped over to the dock to pick up his small fishing pole with the tiny hook. He tied the bait trap to his waist and went back to where the scallop guts were scattered over the water's bottom. He baited up and caught one small fish after another, saving the grunts, chub, and yellow-bellies for Tar Baby and the big white heron that stalked the beach. The silver-sided sand perch and pinfish went into the bait trap. Jody measured each one with his eye as he caught it. None over three inches long went in the trap, and Jody was careful when he took the hook out, making sure not to squeeze the little bodies too tight.

Jeff, in the meantime, had taken the shucked scallops to the house to give to Taffy. When he returned to gather up the shells in the water, he spied a dozen or so blue crabs edging up to get in on the spoils. Jeff slipped back to shore and picked up Jody's dip net lying on the beach.

"Good going, Jeff. You can put 'em right here in the trap."

When Jody finished in the water, he waded ashore and picked up his crutch, leaving Jeff to net the crabs and gather the shells he wanted to keep for Mr. Fulton. Jody had been on his leg now for some time, and, to his surprise, it wasn't hurting all that much. He quickly stifled a feeling of hope—he didn't dare think his leg might be getting better. He had already been disappointed too many times. He wasn't going to be taken in again, he told himself emphatically.

He trudged across the soft sand with the help of his crutch, grateful for the relief from the pain. He bypassed the house and headed for the shed in back that Jeff had cleaned out. He knew that a basin of warm water, soap, a towel and washrag waited for him, along with a change of clothes—compliments of Miss Taffy.

In the shed, he skinned off his wet clothes and draped them over a short clothesline in a corner. He washed and dressed, then went to the back porch, where he rinsed sand from his bare feet in another basin of water.

Taffy was in the kitchen preparing supper. She already had the scallops floured and was snapping string beans. There were smudges of flour on her cheeks when she looked up and smiled. "I can hardly wait to tie into these scallops, Jody. Supper will be ready in about an hour. Your hot water is ready for you in the other room, and I left a space at the table for you to work on cup shells if you want to." She looked at Jody. "How do you feel?"

"I feel fine, Miss Taffy, really. And guess what? Jeff did great out there opening scallops. He's all fired up about it."

Still using his crutch, Jody left the kitchen and stood looking over the big living room. Sunlight, filtering through the avocado tree, sparkled through the clean glass windows. It gave the entire room a diffused glow of soft color. The room itself was larger than the whole of the palmetto shack where he had lived, he realized.

He sat at the table, eased his foot into the purple water, picked up his feather, and went to work on the pile of shells Miss Taffy had set out for him.

≈

"All right, Jeff. Tell us what use Mr. Fulton has for those scallop shells," Jody said through a mouthful of food. They all sat at the table, feasting on fried scallops and new red-skinned potatoes, mounds of green salad, string beans, and baking powder biscuits.

Jeff looked up from his plate. "Well, I told Mr. Fulton I might be trying to work with scallops, now that they're getting bigger. He seemed pleased and told me not to throw away any of the shells because he had a market for them in St. Pete."

"A market for the *shells*?" Jody asked.

"Yes. He said to soak them in bleach water a couple of days to brighten them up, then dry them in the sun. He'll pay us twenty-five cents a bushel if they're in good condition. Said the barnacles will drop off in the bleach water, and a little scrubbing on the top shell would clean off the algae."

"Really!" Taffy exclaimed. "That makes three good reasons for getting out there at low tide and picking up scallops. We can sell the meat *and* the shells and have all we want to eat besides."

"And that's not all," Jeff said, feeling a flush come into his face. "Mr. Fulton also wanted to know if I ever see blue crabs out here. When I told him there was plenty, he told me he could use all the live crabs I could bring in. Told me to make a holding trap. Then, when I got a couple of dozen or more, to put them in crates in layers, with wet sea grass in between. Said he would pay me twenty cents a dozen for them."

Jody came right up out of his chair. "Blue crabs! Twenty cents a dozen!" he whooped. "Now that makes sense to me! And crabs are my department. Finish those other two traps you're workin' on, Jeff, and I'll fill 'em up with crabs every day. Good gravy, what else did Mr. Fulton tell you?"

Jeff grinned, his white teeth showing even whiter in his tanned face.

"That's about it, Jody. But we can all contribute with the crabs. I'm going to bring back another crab net tomorrow, and we'll keep it on the dock for whoever happens to see a crab messing around. I'll finish those two traps after supper so we can anchor them out tomorrow morning. I already got a dozen or so crabs in that other trap."

"Well, I'll be jiggered," Jody squealed. "While we're at it, let's see who can find some more bottles to color. That should give Mr. Fulton something else to think about!"

≈ **27** ≈

Reverend Hammond rapped lightly on Miss Bessie's front door. He stood with his back to the door while he waited, deep in thought about the troubled woman inside. During the past few weeks, she had taken a leave of absence from her work and locked herself away. The preacher was sure that, at this very moment, Miss Bessie was peering through the slit in the curtains to identify her caller before opening the door.

Her behavior was somewhat of a mystery to the preacher. He knew it had to do with Taffy Hansen's disappearance because Miss Bessie was so clearly plagued by guilt—almost to the point of a nervous breakdown. All she talked about was the search party going into Cranes Bog, of all places, looking for the girl. It had become an obsession with her.

He heard a shuffling of slippers on the bare floor as the door opened. He turned to face her. Early morning light shone harshly on the dull pallor of her skin, deepening the lines in her face.

"Reverend Hammond! You've come to bring me news of Taffy! Have they found her?" Her words poured out in an unsteady rush.

"No, Miss Bessie, there's been no news," he answered gently.

The small flame of hope that had shone in her eyes

flickered and died. "I was so in hopes . . ." Her voice trailed off. She turned away.

"As we all were, Miss Bessie."

He followed her into the room where drawn curtains blocked out the light. Mustiness hung in the air. Reverend Hammond regarded the distraught woman closely after she seated herself in a chair beside a small wicker table. Her hands worked nervously as she fiddled with a loose strand of hair. It was obvious Miss Bessie had been sleeping badly. Sunken eyes, peering out from swollen lids, were streaked with red. Two frayed plaits of hair hung down her back in disarray.

The preacher seated himself across the table from her. At his elbow was a bowl of withered flowers. Dead petals littered the table where they had fallen. A cricket sounded somewhere in the woodwork.

"I came to see how you're getting on, Miss Bessie, and, while I'm here, I'll bring you up to date on what's being done about the search. I just talked to Mr. Tanner.

"John Hillard got back last night," he went on, deliberately ignoring the look of scorn that came into Miss Bessie's face. "I thought you'd be interested to know he restocked the launch and set out again this morning to head north."

The preacher reached out to finger some of the crumpled flower petals, nudging them into a neat pile in front of the vase while he waited for Miss Bessie's comment. When none came, he continued.

"The Goddards opened their store last night so John could lay in a fresh supply of groceries. When some of the villagers found out what was going on, they brought fresh fruit and vegetables and baked goods down to the dock for John to take with him."

With a jerk of her head, Miss Bessie rose to her feet. "How can you people be so stupid!" she said scornfully. "Mr. Tanner—he of all people should know better than to invest anything in that worthless drunk. First thing you know, he's going to sell the launch someplace and skip out so he can lay around drunk until the money is gone."

The preacher sighed heavily. "You are forgetting something, Miss Bessie. For the past month, John has been doing his best to find his nephew *and* the Hansen girl. For someone so vitally concerned with that issue, I don't understand your attitude."

He let his breath out slowly. How easily Miss Bessie could get his goat! Each time he called on her, which was quite frequently, she ran the hapless John Hillard into the ground every time his name was mentioned.

Miss Bessie sat again in her chair and began fidgeting. "Tell me, Reverend," she countered. "Do you really have faith in that man?"

"Perhaps at first I didn't," he answered honestly. "But I'm beginning to think differently, as you might, too, when you hear some of the reports I've been getting from Mr. Tanner."

"What reports? All I've heard is that he traveled to God knows where and hasn't found anything."

"That's true."

"Then what do you have to tell me?"

"Just this: John has proven himself both sincere and diligent in his search. All the villagers have recognized this. After all, he didn't have to go anywhere. No one was twisting his arm. And he would have gone whether Mr. Tanner offered him his launch or not. John is doing a real service to this community. You know as well as I do that having two runaways—no matter what their reasons for leaving home—reflects on the entire community. It's important that they be found and brought home to straighten things out. John has covered every inch of the waters to the south, and, even though he found nothing, he's not giving up. He's doing a marvelous job."

The cricket sounded again.

"John Hillard seems to me like a man who is interested in finding his nephew. Not someone who's getting ready to sell his friend's launch and skip out. And don't forget, Miss Bessie, that all the time he's looking for Jody, he is also looking for Taffy."

A haggard look came over Miss Bessie's face as she broke into sobs. She buried her face in her hands and wept. The preacher gently placed his hand on her shoulder.

"I drove her away, Reverend," she wailed. "I drove Taffy away. It's all my fault she's out there now in that dreadful swamp . . . just to get away from me. They've got to find her! They've got to bring her back!"

The preacher stared, bewildered. "There's nothing to be gained by working yourself up like this," he said soothingly.

A strange light burned in the woman's eyes when she looked up at him. "She was so . . . so like my little Jenny, Reverend, . . . so much like my Jenny." Her voice thickened as new tears streamed down her face. "I just can't . . . bear it!"

Reverend Hammond looked at her closely. Jenny, Miss Bessie's little girl who had died before he came to the village. This was the first time he had heard the girl's name on the woman's lips. "Tell me about her," he said softly.

"Wait here."

She went over to the foot of the stairs and returned, carrying a photograph in a gilded frame. She handed it to him.

The preacher looked at the photograph and drew in his breath. He stared, seeing but not quite believing the dramatic similarity of the little girl in the picture frame to Taffy Hansen when she had been a girl.

"You see it, Reverend?"

With effort the preacher took his eyes away and looked into Miss Bessie's anguished face. "Yes," he answered.

Miss Bessie began sobbing again as the preacher looked on helplessly.

"It's . . . it's like my own little Jenny . . . out there . . . lost in that ghastly swamp. Like I had driven her out there myself. . . . My God, Reverend, I can't stand it. . . . It's tearing me to pieces!"

≈

Three weeks later, Cap't. Nate admitted his wife to the psychiatric ward in a hospital in Ft. Myers. She was suffering from a complete nervous breakdown. Later, after she received treatment, Cap't. Nate was told that his wife would never recover if she was permitted to return to her home in Buttonwood Harbor—that she should move to a new community for the rest of her life.

≈ 28 ≈

Taffy raced barefoot down the front steps of the house and walked through the sand until she stood in the shade of the coconut tree. She was dressed in cut-off khaki pants and a sleeveless shirt, and carried a basket in her hand.

She paused for a moment to inspect the three coconuts that had fallen and recently sprouted. Jeff had planted them a short distance from the mother tree. Short green sprigs, not yet formed into character leaves, gleamed bright against the backdrop of white sand.

Nearby, the wooden racks of sieved cup shell mixture were drying in the sun, almost ready to be sorted. Beyond that, lined up next to the house, were tubs of scallop shells curing in bleach water. Taffy walked through neat rows of bottles and other glass objects that they had collected, some already taking on color. But what pleased her most was a section set aside in the back-yard—Jeff's garden, thriving in the sun.

Taffy was on her way to gather shells. The late afternoon sun hung low over the water. She knew the day would soon be out, yet she was unable to pass by the garden without first giving it special attention. From all appearances, the bright green plants seemed to be growing out of nothing more than white beach sand, but of course that was not the case. She remembered the first time Jeff had talked about it.

"How you figgerin' on clearing enough land back there in the jungle to plant a garden?" Jody had inquired.

"Not aiming on clearing any land, Jody. Our garden is going right in the backyard where we can keep an eye on it."

"But that's just dry beach sand out there!"

"Well, it's just dry beach sand now. But it won't be when I get through with it."

Like Jody, Taffy was unable to imagine the barren sand in the backyard being turned into garden soil, no matter what Jeff did to it.

Jeff gave each of them instructions. Taffy was to save all table scraps, including eggshells, coffee grounds, vegetable and fruit peelings, even bones. When Jody fished, he was to save all the trash fish he caught. Jeff would rake in sea grass and spread it out in rows above the high-water mark to cure on the beach. When it was ready, Jeff made it the foundation for a compost. Dried leaves, dead fish, entrails from Jody's big conchs, dead rats Tar Baby brought in each morning, soft coral, jelly-fish, and anything else useful that floated ashore, all went into his compost pile while Taffy and Jody watched with mounting interest.

Day after day, Jeff worked the compost mixture into the sand until the whiteness slowly turned to light gray, then darker shades of gray while he heaped more and more sea grass on top.

"How do you know about this, Jeff?" Jody asked one day. "About a garden on the beach, I mean."

"My grandfather had one out here, right where this one is going now. He planted it the first year the house was built. I helped him treat the soil."

"Really? Your grandfather had a garden, too? Right here? And things grew in it?" Taffy asked.

"Yes."

She remembered how excited she had felt that day.

"What are you going to plant?"

"Well, this is the way I see it, Taffy. I can buy all the vegetables we want for next to nothing in St. Clair, so there's not much use planting more out here."

He stepped over a half-buried log that held the soil in place. "Right here," he announced proudly, "I'm going to plant peanuts. And over there"—he indicated with a sweep of his hand—"I've left plenty of room for watermelon or cantaloupe."

"Boy!" Jody exclaimed. "Watermelon, cantaloupe, and peanuts! What's going in those big cans settin' back there in the shade?"

Jeff grinned. "Mr. Fulton ordered some fruit tree slips from Kilgore's for me, Jody. Fig, orange, and a mango. If they do all right, I'll order some more."

"What are you going to plant up front here?" Taffy wanted to know.

Jeff looked at her searchingly before answering. "I left that for you, Taffy," he replied softly, "for a flower garden. Tell me what you'd like, and I'll get the seeds when I go to Twin Oaks again."

Taffy looked at Jeff, her eyes filled with pleasure. A flower garden! Already she could see the gray-white sand bursting with the colors of spring flowers, and, later, in the hot summer months, with heartier ones—periwinkles, verbenas, marigolds.

"Jeff," she began slowly, "you don't know what this means to me. Back home on Little Placid Bay . . . my grandfather and I . . . well . . . we always had a garden . . . with flowers up front. Always. Every spring, when I was just a little girl, he would take me to town with him to buy his vegetable seeds . . . and he let me pick out the kind of flower seeds I wanted. I'd help him plant them. . . ."

Jeff stood quietly, unable to speak. Her grandfather. It was the first mention she had made of him, except that first day in the lagoon when she had spoken briefly of his death. How grateful he was he had decided on the garden!

Taffy looked at the garden now, as lush and green as any she had ever seen. After the seeds had been planted, she had slipped out each morning to inspect the new developments, eager to greet each green shoot as it came up. She reached down to touch the green watermelon runners spreading over the sand. She counted the yellow blossoms peeking out from under the leaves, and saw green peanut clusters popping up in their section. With special interest, she inspected her round nasturtium plants and snapdragons.

After a while, she straightened up and made her way through clumps of sea oats. She went on until she came to the edge of the bluff, slid down the steep slope, and ran to the water's edge.

A light offshore breeze stirred the gulf waters, bringing in small waves that lapped gently at the shore. She looked around. Thousands of bright-colored little coquinas moved in and out with each receding wave, while seabirds bored their bills into the sand in search of sand fleas.

The sun was setting. Gentle breezes off the gulf cooled her body. She felt tired from the long day's activities, but it was a good feeling just the same. A sense of peace came over her.

There was a real purpose to her life now, she thought. Something she hadn't experienced since leaving home.

To be sure, taking care of Jody before they had met Jeff had been a monumental responsibility, but it was one she had found no satisfaction in. She had never been able to take care of him properly. There had always been his pain, day after day, and the ever dwindling food and medicine supply.

But all that was changed now. She contributed substantially to the income, saved money weekly, and saw to it that Jody did the same. Within the hour now, she would have a hearty meal on the table. Why shouldn't she feel at peace? she asked herself.

As the sun set, she headed for home. She was looking forward to laying out the bright-colored yard goods stacked on the bench in the corner of the living room. This was the curtain material she had had Jeff go into Twin Oaks to get for her—bright yellow Indian Head with small white sprays of flowers in the background. Knowing the transformation the curtains would make in the room, Taffy's hands itched to start making them.

Brightening up the house and making it into a home brought pleasure to Taffy, but, even more, she enjoyed having moments of privacy. How she appreciated a bedroom of her own, and the vine-covered outhouse hidden behind the sea oats! And she cherished moments like this, walking the beach and sorting out her thoughts.

Yes, she told herself, for now she felt at peace. But what was in store for her in the future? Was it possible that sometime, somewhere she might be in a position to go back to school? Sooner or later she would need a high school diploma. And what about Jody's formal education?

She realized that these unanswered questions could easily ruin her frame of mind. She would think about other things. Things like maybe making a batch of cookies to munch on after supper while they sorted cup shells.

She quickened her pace. The day was almost gone. She must hurry home.

≈ **29** ≈

Jody awakened to the lively chatter of mockingbirds in the trees outside his window. He threw the sheet aside and sat up, inspecting his bandage. The white folds lay snug around his calf, neatly in place. No stains showed through.

For the past few weeks, Jody had noticed that definite changes were taking place in his leg—bold, unmistakable changes. The first change he noticed was the condition of his bandages each morning. There was almost no pus, and the bandages were staying in place—an indication that the swelling was down.

Nine days had passed without a setback, Jody told himself happily, still looking at the clean bandage. His leg was definitely healing.

He wiggled into his cut-off pants and rose to his feet, using the back of a chair for support. The familiar pain he always experienced when first getting out of bed jolted him to attention, but he knew it would soon level off to a dull ache and then disappear.

The pail of permanganate water was setting on the stove where Miss Taffy had left it before going fishing with Jeff. He turned on the burner and went back to the living room to work on his cup shells.

Flipping his feather through the shells, he was barely able to contain himself. One thing was clear: *The last piece of catfish fin had finally worked itself out.* One day soon he would be able to walk up the beach, fish in the sound, gather scallops on the grass flats. Last night he dreamed he had climbed the tall avocado tree and picked the fruit. Before long, he was going to jump off the end of the dock and swim ashore.

When he finished soaking his leg, he picked up his hat and headed for the door. He looked back at the cat sleeping on the windowsill. "Come on, Tar, let's go work this leg some in the water."

A dead calm hung in the air. Banks of white clouds reflected on the horizon waters. Two cormorants fished by the dock, appearing and disappearing at the water's surface like a pair of playful otters. A tall white heron stood silent and erect on the dock.

Jody thought about his future and school in the fall. Once he was back on his feet, how would things change? Would Jeff, as the summer turned to fall, think Jody should be back in school? If so, what could he do? Somebody would have to sign him in as his guardian, and the only person qualified to do that was his Uncle John.

No point in borrowing trouble, he reminded himself. So far, he was all right. The way it looked now, it would be some time before he would be ready to return to a classroom anyway. Still, he would have to face the problem someday. He had enough sense to know that he didn't want to go through life with a fourth-grade education.

Maybe that was why Jeff had been bringing books home regularly from the lending library. Jeff had given Jody assignments and checked with him in the evening to make sure he was reading and taking it all in. As far as Jody was concerned, he was learning far more than he had in the classroom back in Buttonwood Harbor. But even so, Jody admitted, he was only filling in a few gaps here and there. A classroom was really the place where he belonged.

He looked around at the peaceful surroundings. He waved at Tar on the beach, then began another trek through the water. When he was tired, he crawled out of the water and stretched out on the sand. He angled his hat over his face and waited for Miss Taffy and Jeff to come home. Within minutes, he was asleep.

≈ 30 ≈

Later that day, Jody told Taffy and Jeff about the improvement in his leg. Taffy stared openmouthed, wondering if she had heard right. "Oh, Jody," she said, "are you sure?"

"Haven't said anything before 'cause I wasn't sure. But now, it's like this . . . my leg doesn't hurt so much anymore . . . and . . . and for over a week now the infection has been drying up."

Jeff dropped to his knees beside Jody and carefully inspected the unbandaged wound. After Jody's trek through the water, the cavity was clean and looked as though there had never been any infection at all. Jeff gently touched the pink flesh, then cupped the palm of his hand over the cavity. There was no heat.

"How long did you say it has been like this, Jody?"

"Over a week. Nine days—I counted them. But before that, it would look clean and pink one day, and ugly and draining pus like crazy the next."

Jeff stood up. "This calls for a celebration!"

"It sure does," Taffy added. "I'll bake a cake. And, Jody, tell us what you'd like more than anything else. Fried chicken? A big baked ham?"

Jody's eyes came alive with anticipation. He thought a moment. "How about a big juicy hamburger with lots of catsup?"

"I have a better idea," Jeff said. "The meat market in

St. Clair has some great-looking steaks. How does that sound, Jody?"

Jody looked first at Jeff, then at Taffy. "Guess I never had a steak. . . ."

"Then you'll have one tonight. We all will. The biggest ones in the store. We'll cook them over the coals."

Jeff needed to get the load of fish to market without further delay, so he picked up his thermos of coffee and took off.

≈

It was midafternoon when he got back. A slow fire burned in the stone hearth beneath the coconut tree, and even before he got to the house he could smell the good odors coming from the kitchen.

Taffy had gone all out. A yellow and white tablecloth, made from the same Indian Head material as the curtains, covered the round table. In the center, graced by two candles, was a low bowl filled with blue lupine. The table gleamed with three white dinner plates Jeff had brought back from the ten-cent store in Twin Oaks.

When he reached the kitchen, he found Taffy taking pans of layer cake out of the oven. For the first time since he had known her, she wasn't wearing khakis. She had on a blue cotton tunic embroidered in white above the smocking. White duck shorts showed just below the tunic hemline. A spray of purple verbenas was tucked snugly in her hair. She slid the pans onto the countertop and turned to look at Jeff.

Jeff's heart stopped. He stood rooted, stunned by the vision before him. He tried to speak, but no words came. His throat was closed, his hands suddenly clammy as he stood with the bag of groceries still in his arms.

Jody's enthusiastic voice broke the spell. He was sitting in a chair in the corner of the kitchen, soaking his leg while he sliced ladyfinger bananas at the counter. He was clad in his best cut-off khaki shorts and shirt, his hair combed neatly in place. "Did you get the steaks, Jeff?"

"Sure thing," Jeff managed with a broad grin.

"This"—Jody indicated with a wave of his hand in the general direction of the layer cakes—"is gonna be a banana cake when we get through with it. I'm fixin' the bananas to put on top of the icing."

He looked inquiringly at Jeff. "Can we see the steaks now?"

≈

Candles cast their soft glow over the dinner table and produced an air of cheerful elegance. The steaks were charred on the outside, bright pink inside. Steaming bowls of potatoes and vegetables lined the table, and in the center sat the creamy white banana cake. Jody cut into his steak with a flourish, tasting the first morsel of meat.

"How is it, Jody?" Jeff asked.

"Super!" Jody responded, his eyes sparkling. "Never ate anything so good! Why don't we do this again tomorrow night?"

≈ **31** ≈

Back in Twin Oaks the next day, Jeff turned east on Main Street and headed for Duffy's Drugs. Jody needed more medicine for the final stages of healing. He had already been to the tavern on the outskirts of town to look for bottles for coloring in the sun. To his delight, the barkeeper had given him several brandy bottles of unusual shapes, along with a promise that he would save more.

With the bottles in a paper bag tucked under his arm, Jeff walked on, his mind back on Pelican Island. He had not been the same since last night, when he had come face to face with his true feelings for Taffy. He found himself going about his work like someone in a trance, totally absorbed with the fascinating person who had ventured to his island and turned his world upside down.

Jeff knew that he couldn't have chosen anyone more unlikely to fall in love with. It was true that Taffy had begun to show signs of recovering from her grandfather's death. But Jeff knew that unhealed wounds lay deep inside. He knew, too, that wounds and thoughts of romance didn't mix. Her mind was not in tune with his. Not to mention the fact that she was only fifteen years old!

But hold on, he reminded himself emphatically, he hadn't *wanted* to fall in love with Taffy. It had just happened. He was in love with her and intended to wait for her until the end of time, if necessary. After all, she would turn sixteen in a few months, and one day her grief would pass. In the meantime, the best he could do was to keep his feelings to himself.

Duffy's Drugs' sign, displayed a few doors up the street, brought Jeff back to reality. Jody's medicine!

The dark-haired girl at the soda fountain was dipping ice cream and the middle-aged lady was at the front register when Jeff entered. He went to the back counter and asked the druggist, Dr. Duffy, for three ounces of permanganate. From the look of interest that came into Dr. Duffy's face, Jeff felt sure the pharmacist remembered him.

After the druggist filled the small medicine vial and handed it to him, Jeff moved back to the aisle where the peroxide was shelved. He had just tucked several bottles in the crook of his arm when he sensed someone behind him.

"Excuse me, young man . . ."

Jeff turned around to face the druggist.

"Yes, sir?"

"About that permanganate. I did give you some careful instructions about handling that poison when you were in here before?"

"Yes, sir. You did."

"Well, I just wanted to remind you to handle it with extreme caution."

"Yes, sir."

Jeff began to breathe a little easier, but Dr. Duffy pressed on. "What are you using it for? Someone in your family treating an infection?"

The pharmacist reached out to wipe a fleck of dust from the shelf. Jeff could feel the blood slowly leaving his face. He searched for a reasonable answer to the question. Finally he spoke. "I'm a fisherman, sir. Make my living from the water, and I'm always stepping on things, like pearl oysters. Fish slime gets into my cuts."

He held up the permanganate. "This stuff takes the soreness out better than anything else."

As Jeff talked, he saw the lines in the druggist's face begin to relax. Then he smiled. "Sooner or later I get to know everybody that comes in my store. You're new around here, son. Where you from?"

Jeff extended his hand. "Jeff Evans, sir. I fish for Mr. Fulton in St. Clair."

The druggist's handshake was firm and friendly. "Glad to make your acquaintance, Jeff."

Jeff drew a deep breath as he went on down the aisle, and Dr. Duffy, apparently satisfied, went back to the rear of the store. Jeff didn't linger. He paid the lady at the cash register and left.

≈ 32 ≈

The first streaks of dawn showed in the east when Jeff and Taffy stepped out of the skiff at the south pass and shoved the bow to shore. From where they stood, it looked as though every sea gull for fifty miles around had congregated on that one strip of white beach to claim territorial rights both on land and in the air. The air was white with flapping wings as the two young people unloaded their gear and waded out into waist-deep water. They were going to try their luck at catching pompano.

Jeff had never caught a pompano and doubted he would know one if he saw one, but then Taffy had never caught one either. Jody had, but right now he was back at the dock observing his penned-up crabs that were ready to shed their shells. There were three dozen or more of them in this premolting condition, ready to "put on a show," as Jody had described it, by backing out of their shells. More than anything else, Jody wanted to know about their needs at this time: whether they would be safe in the trap after discarding their shells or whether those that hadn't yet gone through the process would attack and begin to feed on them.

Timing was a big factor in dealing with soft-shelled crabs, Jody had learned, and, because Mr. Fulton was willing to pay a good price for them, Jody saw to it that he got only the best. The crabs that shed their shells now would be delivered and quick-frozen today, before any hint of a new film of shell had begun to form.

"I almost wish we had waited for another time to come down here, Jeff, so Jody could have come with us. He's the one that knows how to catch these things," Taffy said. She baited her hook with a small sand flea crustacean and threw out her line as Jody had instructed.

Several nights earlier, Jody had brought up the subject of catching pompano. "Be around all summer, so we may as well get started on seeing what we can do about 'em," he had announced with his usual enthusiasm. "Don't know all that much about 'em, but I lucked me some when I was on some of my jaunts away from home. There should be some out here in this gulf water, especially around the passes."

"Guess you know they bring a fancy price," Taffy had added to Jeff, "besides being the best eating fish in the water."

"Don't know anything about them except what you've been telling me," Jeff answered. "But if you think they're down there at the pass, what are we waiting for?"

Now Jeff nudged his bait gently. Just then a fish grabbed it and took off. Jeff set the hook and backed into shore, Taffy right on his heels.

"What is it, Taffy? Is it a pompano?" Jeff asked as Taffy netted it.

"A real pompano, Jeff, and a nice one. Run about three pounds." She ran her fingertips down the belly of the flashy gold and white fish. "See how it curves out down here? Not flat at the bottom like a jack. You just caught us a fish worth about fifty cents. Now let's get back out there and catch some more. Boy! This is real fishing!"

For three hours, the pompano continued to snap up bait, charging the air at the south pass with nerve-tingling excitement and shouts of unexpected delight as they were brought ashore, one after another.

"I counted thirty-eight of 'em, Jeff," Taffy exclaimed breathlessly when they were putting their gear away. "Aren't they beautiful?" She picked one up in her hands and examined it closely. "Most of 'em run around two pounds apiece, and they're all salable size except maybe four of 'em." She looked up. "Won't Jody be surprised?"

"No more than I am, Taffy. Gosh! What a fantastic day! I can't believe it! Pulling those fish in is like scooping up pieces of gold out of the water! And we have those four to eat besides! You don't think this is just beginner's luck, do you?"

"No—it's like Jody said. These pompano have probably been hanging around the pass ever since the water warmed up. Bet we can catch this many or more anytime we want to when the tide is right."

≈

Taffy was unusually quiet on the way home. She sat on the bow and looked over the railing. The morning sun brought out the richness of her skin and hair. Jeff looked at her. "What are you thinking?"

Without looking up, she reached out and picked up her hat. She took her time angling it over her head to keep the sun out of her eyes. "Lots of things," she answered thoughtfully. "Like catching pompano this morning. Seems like everything we do is enjoyable as well as profitable. When I left home, I never expected to find peace of mind—how I hated leaving home!"

She drew a deep breath and went on. "I still miss home, and I'll always miss my grandfather, but at least now I feel some peace here with you and Jody, doing the things we do."

Jeff sat quietly; a new rush of love came over him. As the silence stretched out, he spoke. "What do you like best about what we do?"

"It's not so much what we do, I guess. It's more a feeling of everybody working as a team and all of us looking out for each other. We all need each other, one way or another. It's that need that binds us. But to answer your question better, I guess I like the time we all spend around the table after supper, sortin' cup shells and talking about the day. It's just a pleasant feeling of letting our hair down and forgetting our problems for a little while when we're all together like that—especially now that Jody's leg is healing. I wish it could go on like this forever, but I know it can't. Guess that's what I was thinkin', Jeff."

Jeff stopped poling. He was thinking how simple it would be to tell her he loved her, to ask her to marry him and go on living on the island, but he couldn't. With effort, he cleared his throat and asked, "Why do you say that?"

"You know we can't stay here indefinitely. Not Jody or me. It was different when Jody was sick. None of us was thinking about anything then except gettin' him straightened out and back to health. But now, with his leg on the mend, it's time to start thinkin' about other things."

Jeff felt his stomach muscles knotting. The discussion, so warm only moments ago, had taken a very unfavorable turn.

"Start thinkin' about what other things?"

"About looking ahead, Jeff. I'll be sixteen 'fore long. When I'm sixteen, the welfare people won't mess with me anymore. But Jody's only twelve. If a truant officer was to get wind of him not being in school, they'd escort him right back to Buttonwood Harbor and see that he stays there.

"So far, we've been lucky," she hurried on. "Nobody around here knows anything about us. But someday somebody might come poking around and start wondering, and then we could all be in a jam, including you, Jeff. Jody worries about this, too, saying he never wants to leave the island, and that he doesn't care if he never sees another human being besides us. That's why he's been so willing to study the textbooks you've brought home. He knows he's the one the school authorities will be concerned with."

Taffy was right, of course. In fact, Jeff had been having the same thoughts, but he had been reluctant to put them into words. Now that Taffy had brought it out into the open, and because Jeff had no reasonable answers, he stalled for time. "What do you tell Jody when he talks about these things?"

"Nothing much. I just tell him things will work out somehow because I don't know what else to say. Then he turns those big, soulful eyes of his on me and begs me not to leave him, that he couldn't stand it if we were ever separated. I've told him over and over that I won't leave him, that we'll stick together no matter what. And we will, too."

Jeff couldn't trust himself to speak. He turned away, trailing the oar again. Taffy went on. "If Jody is ever found out and sent back to Buttonwood Harbor, I'll go with him. I'll see that somebody takes responsibility for him besides his uncle, somebody like Mr. Tanner or Reverend Hammond, and I'll stick around the village myself to watch out for him as long as he needs me. If that doesn't work out, we can always take off again."

A tremor had crept into her voice. Jeff looked at her. She sat like a figure in a painting. He knew there was no way he could feel more miserable than at that moment.

"That may not sound like much of a solution, but it's all I have. Jody means too much to me now to ever turn my back on him. Besides, he saved my neck that day in the swamp with the rattlers. The least I can do is to see that the situation with his uncle is cleared up somehow. I owe him that."

Jeff knew it was time to say something. He drew a deep breath to try to calm himself.

"What you've been saying is true enough, Taffy. I've had the same thoughts all along. But the way it stands now, Jody couldn't sit in a classroom if he wanted to. He still needs hot water soakings three times a day, and he's not able to get around all that well on his own. Besides, there's three more months of summer ahead of us. If anybody should find out about you two being out here with me, they wouldn't give it a second thought."

"I know that, but someday this thing with Jody will have to be straightened out, and that's what worries me. That's why I keep thinkin' about having to leave here. I feel the same as Jody: I hate the thought of going back, now that my grandfather isn't there. But when I try to think of a way out, I always come back to the same thing: Jody's Uncle John is his only kin. Nobody else can take over without his say-so, and this whole business of ever finding a sensible solution has to start right back there in Buttonwood Harbor, like it or not."

Taffy looked away. When she spoke again, it was as if she was speaking to herself. "Sometimes I wish that Jody and I could just move on a couple of hundred miles more and forget the whole thing."

Jeff responded quickly. "It's not just your problem, Taffy. We're all in this together. After watching and worrying about Jody all this time, seeing him fight his battle with his leg and never complaining . . . well . . . I've come to love the kid like one of my own brothers. Don't know yet what I can do, but you can bet I'm not going to let him go anywhere if I can help it."

A softness came into Taffy's eyes when she looked at Jeff. It gave him the encouragement he needed to go on. "There's more, Taffy. That day in the lagoon when I found you and Jody . . . well . . . something happened to me. . . ."

His voice thickened. "It was something I couldn't explain even to myself at the time. I looked at you standing there barefoot in those old khakis with your hat jammed down over your face, glaring holes through me. . . ."

Before Taffy could respond, Jeff hurried on. "I thought you were the most beautiful girl I had ever seen."

Jeff pulled in his stomach and squared his shoulders, stretching himself to his full height. Had he really said those things? He wondered where his courage had come from. He could hear his own heartbeat. He stared at the water, determined to go on. "Taffy, what I'm about to say now is something I've never said to a girl before. I'm not sure how to say it right. But . . . I . . . well, I guess I fell for you like a ton of bricks."

The stillness at that moment was absolute. Nothing stirred. Even the skiff was motionless on the water.

"Since then," Jeff continued, "I've come to love you more than I ever thought possible. I know you are too young for this kind of thinking—but someday, I'd like to marry you. We could go on living here like we are now, Jody included. . . ." His voice trailed off.

Taffy made no comment, nor did she stir from her position on the bow.

"I had to say this, Taffy, because I can't even imagine myself without you and Jody. Nothing would have any meaning."

At last, Taffy stirred. She kept her eyes averted. "Guess I never thought much about . . . about gettin' married, Jeff . . . I never had a boyfriend. . . ."

Jeff set the boat in motion, wondering. Had he spoken too soon? Did she think him a fool to expect her to marry him? Had it sounded like a marriage of convenience that provided a way out for both her and Jody? He didn't have to wonder for long.

"Jeff, like you said," she responded softly, "I'm not ready for this kind of thinking. I'm thinking of you more like a good friend, a special kind of friend. For now, I'd just like to leave it that way."

Relief flooded through him. The intimacy of his confession had not changed their relationship. Besides, he told himself, the gate was still open—she hadn't turned him down! He was still her friend. He couldn't ask for more.

≈ **33** ≈

Mr. Tanner closed his ledger with a resigned sigh. The summer slump on fishing was beginning to take effect. His fish house was barely making expenses, but, because of the good winter season behind him, he was not concerned for himself. He had money tucked away in the bank in Bayview, and he would survive, just as he always had. It was the fishermen he was thinking about. Most of the money they had earned during the mullet spawning season had already been turned over to the bank to pay off last year's mortgages. It would be nip and tuck for them for the rest of the summer. The old man knew that a lot of the men would not make it without another stake from the bank.

The telephone at his elbow sounded. He looked at the irritating instrument a moment before picking it up. "Tanner Fish Co., Tanner speaking."

The operator informed him that it was a collect call from a John Hillard at St. Clair. Yes. Mr. Tanner would accept the call.

"Mr. Tanner." John Hillard's voice boomed out in the small confines of the office. *"I've found Jody and Taffy!"*

Mr. Tanner slowly came up out of his swivel rocker. A flush spread over his face. "Wait a minute, John. Give that to me again. *Did you just say you found Jody and Taffy?"*

"Yes, sir. About a half hour ago. Haven't made contact with 'em yet, but it's them all right."

The old man sank back in his chair. "Both of them! Gad, John, I'm speechless. Are they all right?"

"Apparently so, sir. Jody was limpin' some, but other than that, they both looked fit enough to me."

"Well, tell me more. Where are they? Where are you? This place called St. Clair—never heard of it."

"It's a small village just south of Tampa Bay. I saw Jody and the Hansen girl through binoculars. They're on an island in the gulf about three or four miles out."

"Tampa Bay! That far from home, eh? Start at the beginning, John. Tell me why you haven't made contact with them."

The old man chewed on the stem of his pipe and listened while John talked first about a net fisherman he had met in Lemon Bay. The man, named Amos, knew Jody from Jody's earlier travels. Amos figured the boy might have holed up in an old abandoned homestead place up the coast a ways. On an island called Pelican Island on the charts. A place Amos knew Jody had been to before.

"The closer I got to that island, the more nervous I started gettin', sir. And instead of just barging in, I decided to check things out first. Hid low on the boat and got out the binoculars. There was a rowboat and a skiff tied up at the dock. The skiff looked like Jody's. Then I saw Jody come out of the house and head for the water."

"You said he was limping?"

"Yes, sir. He was limpin' and had a bandage on his leg. But he looked good from what I could make out. Looked like he might have put on a little weight.

"The Hansen girl showed up from behind the house about thirty minutes later," John said. "At first I thought she was another boy, until she took off her hat. It was her hair, sir. A dead giveaway. Nobody has hair like that 'cept the Hansen girl."

"Did you see anyone else around?"

"Yes, sir. While I was keepin' a lookout, I saw another skiff being poled up the shoreline by a husky-lookin' feller, maybe in his late teens. Looked like he was carrying a load of something, but I couldn't make out what it was. When he got up there to the dock, he just tied up the skiff and joined the other two. It looks like this guy is a friend, and that's what made me nervous, sir. Guess I'm the last person Jody wants to see right now, if he's doin' all right on his own, and . . . well . . . I plain don't know how to handle it from now on. . . ."

Mr. Tanner sat very still, his pipe poised halfway to his mouth. John had a point there, all right. He glanced up at the clock on the wall. Ten fifteen.

"John, listen to me. When we get off the phone, you go somewhere out of sight. But keep your binoculars on that island. I'll get Jonas's brother to take care of the fish house for a few days, and Jonas and I will meet you at the St. Clair wharf, say sometime around dusk. We'll figure out the rest from there. All right?"

"Yes, sir, Mr. Tanner, and thanks. I appreciate it. Sure will be a load off me to have you here."

≈ **34** ≈

"Hey! I almost forgot to tell you and Miss Taffy something excitin' that happened to me this morning out in the water," Jody said to Jeff, with a little more than his usual degree of enthusiasm.

"What was that?" Jeff asked.

He turned to look at the boy seated at the round table. The glow from the lamps rested pleasantly on his bare, dark torso, now glistening faintly with perspiration from the warm night air.

"It was just offshore of the dock when I first saw it—a big dark mass moving through the water. I thought it was a patch of cloud overhead till I saw the ripples, then a flipper or two cuttin' the water. Figgered it was a school of devilfish from the color, but they were too far out to be sure. Then all of a sudden one of 'em came up out of the water not fifty feet away. Startled the liver out of me. Seemed to just hang there over the water like it was floatin' on air, and when it came down flat on its belly, it sounded like a cannon goin' off. It was the biggest one I ever saw. No kiddin'—that monster would have run a couple of tons!"

"Devilfish?" Jeff asked, his eyes wide with interest. "A couple of tons? What's a devilfish?"

"Manta ray, if you want to get technical. Called devilfish because they look so weird. Got things on their faces that look like horns, and a long tail in back, and they're black on top."

"Manta ray," Jeff said, as if to himself. "Aren't they dangerous? What would happen if you were to come face to face with one?"

"Nothin'," Jody answered solemnly. "Couldn't hurt you if they wanted to."

"Oh. I thought all rays were dangerous."

"No, just the stingarees."

"But that ain't . . . isn't . . . all," Jody went on, casting his eyes at Taffy, who was helping Jeff clear the supper dishes from the table. "After that bunch of devilfish passed by, I looked toward the point and saw another dark patch comin' my way. This was closer to shore and moving slower. If I had stayed where I was in neck-deep water, they would have come right up on me. I started backing to shore 'cause I didn't want to be caught short, in case they turned out to be a mess of sharks."

Taffy looked at Jody quickly. "Weren't you getting a little spooked?"

"Well, a little, maybe."

"What happened then?"

"Well, I was in waist-deep water when they got close enough for me to make 'em out. More devilfish. Thousands of 'em no bigger across than a washtub, so I just stood there and watched 'em go by."

"You just *stood* there? Why didn't you go to shore to watch?" Jeff asked incredulously.

"Oh, I backed up some, but 'fore long I was surrounded with 'em. I was kinda fascinated 'cause they weren't afraid of me—like I was an old piling or somethin'. They didn't touch me with their flippers, just swam around me and went on their way. It made me feel good while it lasted, like they was thinkin' I belonged there in the water, too. For a minute, I even thought about swimmin' with 'em."

A sheepish look came into Jody's eyes. "Does that sound dumb to you?" he asked no one in particular.

"Not to me it doesn't," Taffy answered thoughtfully.

"Well it does to me, Jody," Jeff retorted. "Fraternizing with rays with horns and long tails. You sure there's no stingers on those things?"

"Positive."

≈

Taffy, at the sink in the kitchen, slid the last of the supper dishes into a pan of soapy water. She reached for a bowl of oranges on the counter, then withdrew her hand convulsively when she heard an unfamiliar sound outside. She jerked her head up, listening. The sound, alien at first, was repeated. Someone was knocking at the door of the front porch!

Fear exploded inside her. She stood transfixed, staring at the bare wall. Thoughts came at her like a swarm of bees: Flee from the kitchen! Lose herself in the darkness! Hide in the thicket of sea oats! She bolted past the counter and reached for the latch to the back door. All sanity had left her.

Just then, Jody's nervous cough brought her to a halt. She slowly turned her head and looked into the next room.

Jeff stood tall in the center of the well-lit living room, a jar of unsorted cup shells forgotten in his hands. Muscles bunched in his jaw.

"You two," he commanded in a low, curt voice, "stay where you are. It's probably some stranger on the water looking for directions."

With that, he turned on his heels and left the room, trailing silence in his wake. He opened the screen door and slipped outside.

Taffy moved waiflike into the living room and, taking

Jody's hand in hers, sat down beside him. He looked at her with large, frightened eyes. Neither one spoke.

The house had suddenly become deathly quiet.

≈

When Jeff stepped outside the door, he saw, in a small patch of light, the shrunken figure of an old man standing at the foot of the steps. He was dressed in work clothes and held a cap in his hands. Wisps of white hair showed in the semidarkness. He extended a gnarled hand and spoke in a voice that seemed to belong to a far younger person than the one Jeff was staring at.

"I'm Thomas Tanner. Fish dealer from a small village south of Ft. Myers."

Jeff was stunned. Hairs prickled at the back of his neck. He tried to speak but nothing came out. Thomas Tanner! Was this the same Mr. Tanner who was Taffy and Jody's friend?

Without thinking Jeff glanced back at the house. He saw the wide expanse of open windows, the brightly lit rooms. There was no doubt that the old man had seen everything. With sinking heart, Jeff knew that they were trapped.

He knew he had to say something, to introduce himself as any well-manner person would, but he could only stare while his mind churned helplessly. With effort, he spoke in a calm voice. "Jeff Evans, sir. This is my home. I'm a fisherman. Can I help you?"

As he spoke, he found himself edging away from the house, leading the man out of earshot of the two inside. He had to keep his wits about him. If anything could be salvaged, he intended to find out what it was.

"Yes, Jeff. To make a long story short, our people from Buttonwood Harbor have spent eight anxious weeks looking for two of our young people who disappeared from the village." His voice became thick with emotion. "It seems I've finally found them."

The two people stood in silence. The old man had said it all, and each word had fallen on Jeff like a hammer blow.

As he studied Mr. Tanner, Jeff could see, in the faint light, moisture glistening in the man's eyes. This Mr. Tanner from Buttonwood Harbor apparently loved the two inside very much. Still . . .

"Please, sir, let me say something before we go inside," Jeff ventured cautiously.

"Of course. What is it?"

Another silence fell on them while Jeff groped for words. "I'm finding this a little difficult. . . ."

"Take your time, son," the old man said gently.

"Well, first, let me say this—I've heard both Taffy and Jody speak very highly of you."

He hesitated, then continued. "But they're neither of them going to be very pleased about you showing up here like this. You are expecting to take them back home, and they are not ready to face the things they left behind."

Jeff drew a deep breath and plunged on. "They're happy where they are, and if there's any way this matter can be worked out without putting them through any further unhappiness, I trust you'll do your best to find it."

Mr. Tanner turned away. He tucked his hat under his arm and looked into the darkness thoughtfully. "We have spent many long, sleepless nights hoping and praying those two kids had come to no harm." He looked at Jeff again. "In the meantime, a lot of things have happened back in our village—things that are bound to change both their lives."

The old man looked toward the house. "I didn't come here to create more unhappiness, Jeff. You see, I love those two kids, and right now all I want is to see for myself that they are all right. We'll figure out the rest when the time comes. Fair enough?"

Jeff felt sheepish. "I meant no offense, sir."

"Nor was any taken."

≈

When Jeff stepped into the house, all the confidence he had felt outside suddenly fell away. Two pairs of eyes stared in shocked disbelief at both him and the old man trailing behind.

The tension was an enormous force, spreading itself into every corner of the room. Not knowing what else to do, Jeff seated himself on a bench at the far wall, leaving the old man alone in the middle of the room.

No one spoke as Mr. Tanner looked searchingly from one face to another, his own face flushed with emotion. Finally, he spoke. "I've never been so glad to see anyone as I am you two youngsters right now."

The simple statement, soft-spoken and with genuine sincerity, had a disarming effect on Taffy. It brought a trace of a smile to her lips. Mr. Tanner crossed the room and took her hand in his. "You're even prettier than you were before, Taffy."

He turned to Jody. "Tell me, son, how's your leg?"

Jody, still shocked and afraid, kept his eyes averted. His lower lip trembled.

"You know, Jody," Mr. Tanner said, "everybody in the village knew *you* would be all right, no matter where you were. You've quite a reputation for taking care of yourself on the water, and going to a lot of interesting places in that skiff of yours."

Jody fidgeted with his hands.

"It wasn't your disappearance that had us upset. It was your leg that worried us. Miss Daisy told us what kind of shape it was in when you took off."

192

Jody slowly looked up. Mr. Tanner had succeeded in stirring up a spark of pride. He managed a thin smile. "It's better now, sir."

The response Mr. Tanner had gotten from his two friends, however lukewarm, encouraged him considerably.

Jeff took advantage of the moment. He got up from his bench and pulled out a chair for Mr. Tanner. "Make yourself comfortable, sir. I'll make coffee."

The old man sank into the chair gratefully. He dug in his pockets for his pipe and tobacco just as the black cat came out from under the table and jumped in his lap.

"Well hello there, old boy. I'm happy to see you, too."

Taffy picked up a clamshell for Mr. Tanner to use as an ashtray and placed it on the table beside him. She sat back in her chair. "How did you find us, Mr. Tanner?"

Jeff, pouring boiling water in the top of the coffeepot, hesitated, listening, the kettle poised in his hand.

It was some time before Mr. Tanner answered. He finished with his pipe before looking up. "Seems like that's a long story, Taffy. Guess I'd better start at the beginning. A lot of things have happened back home since you left. Things we should talk about."

In a quiet, understated manner, the old man first talked about how different members of the community had looked into what could be done to keep Taffy in the village, where she belonged.

He leaned forward in his chair to look at her. "Did you really think we would sit by and allow Miss Bessie to send you away?"

Taffy shivered involuntarily.

"Between the time of your grandfather's death and his burial, we turned up three families willing to provide you with a good home." A smug grin of satisfaction showed at the corners of the old man's mouth. "Then we

193

went over Miss Bessie's head and got the approval of Judge Harrison."

Mr. Tanner blew a cloud of thin smoke into the air before going on. "So you see, child, you needn't have left at all."

Taffy squirmed. Two months ago, she would have been greatly relieved to have heard these words, but not now. Except for her grandfather's peaceful little shack on the shore of Little Placid Bay, her village no longer held the appeal it once had. "I didn't know. . . . No one told me."

"I should have told you myself, but because you were in shock over your grandfather's death, I figured it could wait a few days."

Jeff came out of the kitchen carrying a steaming cup of coffee. He set it down beside Mr. Tanner and went back for cream and sugar, along with two of Taffy's muffins.

Mr. Tanner looked pleased. "I'm a tired old man, Jeff. I needed this," he responded. "Thanks. There's more, Taffy," he went on. "Miss Bessie is no longer with the welfare agency."

Taffy's face came alive. Her lips parted as if to speak, but nothing came out. She stared at the old man in silence.

"As a matter of fact, Miss Bessie no longer lives in the village. She and Cap't. Nate put their home up for sale some time back and moved inland to be closer to Miss Bessie's people. Cap't. Nate is farming now instead of fishing."

"Why, Mr. Tanner?" Taffy asked, barely able to keep her voice under control.

Mr. Tanner explained the gradual breakdown that had finally forced Miss Bessie to give up her job and move away. Taffy, turning back to her own thoughts, barely heard him.

Total freedom! It was as if a great burden had been

lifted. She smiled inwardly, grateful for this bit of news the village patriarch had brought.

But there were still Jody and his miserable uncle to worry about . . .

"You asked how I found you and Jody, Taffy, and, as I said, it's a long story."

Mr. Tanner talked about the long search and the disappointment after it ended. A small grin played at the corners of his mouth. "Sure did a good job of giving us the slip, Taffy. Like the boys on the search said, 'She just ain't nowhere . . . plain out vanished into thin air.' When we get around to it, I'd like to know how you managed it."

He turned his attention to Jody, who sat very still, eyes glued to the floor as if waiting for the death sentence to fall. Jody felt the old man's eyes on him and flinched inwardly.

"Your uncle was with us all during the search, Jody. No one knew it at the time, but he was looking, not for Taffy, but for you. He told me after the search ended that you had disappeared, too."

Mr. Tanner looked for a reaction that wasn't long in coming. Jody's head jerked up, and his eyes flashed with resentment. Did Mr. Tanner really believe that, he wondered?

"I turned up missin' lots of times, Mr. Tanner. My uncle never went lookin' for me before. Why should he go out lookin' for me this time?" he countered.

"I can't say what prompted his actions at this point, son," Mr. Tanner replied gently. "He didn't confide in me as to the *whys*, but if I were to venture a guess, I'd say he was suffering from an acute case of the 'guilts' and decided it was time to do something about it."

He talked on about John's decision to continue with the search alone, and Mr. Tanner's part in it.

"You see, Jody, I recognized something in your uncle I

195

hadn't seen in a long time. For one thing, his whole attitude changed almost overnight. One day he was the shifty-eyed drunk, the next the clearheaded, neat-appearing man we used to know. It was like the snap of a finger. The look of hopelessness was gone. He seemed so determined, so sincere about the plans for his search, so *alive,* I couldn't help but take notice. While he was at it, I wanted him to find both of you."

Mr. Tanner outlined John's moves from the beginning up to the present while the room, except for the drone of the old man's soft voice, became more quiet all the time. No one moved.

"As I said before, Jody, no one knows exactly what motivated your uncle to do what he did, but one thing I *can* say for a certainty—he has not touched a drop of alcohol since the first day of the search."

But Jody's face had closed. The more Mr. Tanner talked, the tighter the web was being drawn around him. He knew where the discussion, with its implications, was leading. Mr. Tanner would expect him to be overjoyed with this news about his uncle, but all he felt was a desperate need to find some way out of his own misery. He didn't understand his uncle's sudden concern or what he was trying to prove, but none of it mattered anymore. For Jody, there was no turning back. His faith in his uncle was gone, his scars too deep.

Mr. Tanner had finished talking and sat back in his chair, relaxing with his coffee. He ate a muffin while Jody and Taffy sat in silence across the table.

Finally, Jody looked up with tears in his eyes. "Why can't he leave me alone, sir? Why does he have to come all the way up here looking for me? And what does he expect me to do, now that he's found me?"

Mr. Tanner didn't answer. He put his coffee aside and studied the boy's face.

"Where is he now? My Uncle John?"

The old man slowly rose to his feet and went over to the boy. He placed a withered hand on Jody's shoulder.

"At the St. Clair wharf with Jonas," Mr. Tanner said gently. After a pause he went on. "I know how you feel, son, but this meeting with your uncle will have to take place sooner or later. It may as well be now."

Jody made no comment.

"I'm going over there now and bring your uncle back with me. In the meantime, try to get things sorted out in your mind. Try to understand there's no reason for tears. I'm here to help you, not to make matters worse. Keep that in mind, Jody." He turned toward the door. "I'll be back shortly."

Jeff came out of the kitchen and reached for a flashlight on the mantel. "I'll go with you, sir."

The two left the room. Within minutes, the soft chug of an engine was heard floating over the night air.

≈

Jody steeled himself for the meeting with his uncle. He slumped even farther down in his chair and glared, unseeing, at the flame in the lamp. He remembered the last time he had seen him—the bloated, unshaven face where he lay on his bed, oblivious to the world about him or his nephew stuffing his belongings into a canvas bag. Jody already knew how he would deal with *him*. In all probability, regardless of what the old man had said, his uncle's mind and body had burned out long ago. There would be the shaky hands, the pasty flesh, the empty eyes. His Uncle John would be a pushover. It was Mr. Tanner he had to worry about, and Jody wasn't at all sure how to deal with him.

He looked at Taffy with brooding eyes. "I hate him, Miss Taffy! I hate my Uncle John and I'm not going back to live with him no matter what he's done or what Mr. Tanner says!"

He sat taut, knowing his voice would break if he said another word. Taffy drew him to her, comforting him like a mother with a child.

"Listen to me, Jody," she said gently. "I don't think you're seeing things the way they really are. After all, the only thing changed is that your uncle finally tracked you down, which in the long run doesn't mean all that much. You're twelve years old. He can't drag you back home and make you live with him."

She took a paper napkin out of her shirt pocket and wiped at a tear on his cheek.

"He'll try, Miss Taffy, and so will Mr. Tanner."

"Yes, they will, Jody, but with your uncle's track record, they won't get very far, even if he has been sober for two months. He has to make more of a showing than that. Besides, neither he nor Mr. Tanner knows anything about what's happened to you since you left home, and it seems to me like we've got plenty to talk about when they get back."

"Like what, Miss Taffy?" Jody asked with renewed interest.

Taffy didn't answer. She got up and slowly paced back and forth in front of the fireplace, hands stuffed deep in the back pockets of her khaki pants.

"Look, Jody, you just leave that part of it to me and Jeff. After all, we're all in this together. All you have to do is hash it out with your uncle as you see fit. And while we're waitin' for them to get back, I want you to pull yourself together so you can talk up to him man to man without tears and with as little anger as you can manage. All right?"

Jody squared his shoulders. He set his jaw. A trace of a smile found its way to his lips.

"All right, Miss Taffy. I'll do my best."

≈ **35** ≈

Jeff, John, and Mr. Tanner came through the front door in single file. Jeff, bringing up the rear, pulled out chairs for the other two, then excused himself and headed for the kitchen to make fresh coffee. The man Jody saw following Mr. Tanner was like a stranger, tall and lean in clean khakis. Light from the lamps flickered softly over the clean-shaven face that smiled shyly as clear gray eyes rested on Jody's face.

Just for a moment, like something out of a science fiction novel, Jody felt he had been transported back into another era.

But no! he stormed silently to himself. It wasn't like that! What he was seeing was nothing more than an illusion. Nothing had changed. Underneath the clean clothes he would still find his pathetic Uncle John.

He slowly rose to his feet. Limping to the table where his uncle and Mr. Tanner sat, he stood before his uncle and extended his hand. "I'm sorry you went to so much trouble to find me, sir," he said in a dignified manner.

John had some difficulty finding his voice, but he finally spoke, using almost the same words Mr. Tanner had used before. "I've never been so glad to see anyone in my life, Jody."

Jody, not wanting to hear more, limped back to his chair and sat down. John was plainly ill at ease. He fingered the clamshell ashtray, looking first into the flame in the lamp, then over at Jody. His nephew's face was unreadable. Finally, John spoke. "I'm mighty glad to see you looking so fit."

"Yes, sir."

Another awkward silence fell while John groped for words. He squirmed in his chair.

"This may sound insincere, Jody . . . but you have to believe it. . . . I love you very much. I always have. . . . All the time I was drinkin' I loved you . . . and hated myself for what I was doing to you. . . ."

He shoved the ashtray aside and looked directly into Jody's face. "It's been sixty-five days, Jody. Kept track of every one of them, and I feel like a new man. A human being. Like someone who died and came back to life. Don't expect you to understand about these things, but I will tell you something you *can* understand. It all happened right after I found out about your trouble with the catfish fin. Gus told me what that doctor said, and it hit me like a ton of bricks. For the first time in years, I actually saw myself as I really was. It was like a light had suddenly been turned on in my head."

Jody listened, but he wouldn't look at his uncle. He stared at the tabletop, arms folded in front of him.

"Night after night on the water," John went on, "the same dream kept coming back to me while I slept. I had found you and brought you home. We were friends again like we used to be. Then I'd wake up and press on, farther and farther into my search. And now . . . now that I've found you . . . now that I'm really sitting here across the table from you, I swear"—he held up his hand in a gesture of sincerity—"I'll make it up to you, Jody . . . somehow. . . ."

Jody still wouldn't look at his uncle.

"All I ask is a chance, Jody. . . ."

John's voice trailed off. Jody looked up then, and a coldness flashed in his dark, brooding eyes. He rose to his feet. "It's too late, Uncle John," he lashed out. "I'm not going back with you. If you force me to, I'll leave again, so you may as well save us both the trouble. I don't believe that you won't go back to drinkin'. I don't believe it when you say you love me. I don't believe anything you say. I never want to see the hut you call home again. I wish you had just stayed there and left me alone."

Before he finished, Jody's voice broke. Tears welled up in his eyes. He sat down slowly, still glaring.

John felt as if he had been struck in the face. He wasn't prepared for his nephew's open hostility.

The room was still again. Taffy, seated beside Jody, neither spoke nor looked up. In the kitchen, Jeff had finished making the coffee. When he'd heard Jody's outburst, he had left the stove and stood in the doorway. Now Mr. Tanner rose to his feet. He moved over to the table, anger showing in his face.

"You're being unfair, son. Your uncle has spent many a long hour looking for you. If he didn't love you, he wouldn't have bothered with you at all. He's been through hell pulling himself together. He's a man again, and I for one have faith in him. Seems to me you could at least be civil, Jody."

"Yes, sir," Jody mumbled grudgingly.

"Your uncle is giving you a chance to go back to a decent life. There's no reason to carry around unpleasant memories. It's time to bury them and start over."

He touched Jody under the chin, lifting his face. "Besides, it's time to settle down. When your leg is ready, you'll be needing to get back in school."

The old man's words hung in the air, settling over Jody like a black cloud. He was miserable. He could feel all his reserve draining away. He stumbled to his feet again. "Please, Mr. Tanner . . . sir," he pleaded. "You've always been kind to me. . . . I've not forgotten any of it . . . and I

201

don't want to have to say anything now that might sound ungrateful or disrespectful . . . but . . . but my mind is made up. . . . I'll not ever live with my uncle again."

He backed away from the table, knowing the tears could not be held in check any longer. He reached for his crutch leaning against the wall behind the yellow curtain and stumped out of the room.

Mr. Tanner slumped into the nearest chair, looking skeptically at John. No one spoke until Taffy looked into the faces of the two men. Her eyes burned with unnatural brightness.

"Neither of you would have any way of knowing this, but Jody is just now beginning to recover from a sickness he's had for weeks. His leg will probably bother him for the rest of his life. In his condition, he is not ready for this kind of badgering. Besides, he never intended to go back to Buttonwood Harbor when he left, so this outburst is not something that just came up. He meant what he said."

Both men, deep in thought, stared at the floor. Finally Mr. Tanner spoke. "Tell us about Jody, Taffy."

"Well, first I can tell you that Jody and I didn't leave together, as you may have thought. We met by chance in Cranes Bog. . . ."

Taffy talked about the rattlers on the water, about Jody's bonfire on the shell bar and the long trip up the coastline. She gave special emphasis to Jody's painful and stubborn infection, and the important part Jeff had played in the whole matter.

"Jody's infection didn't get to the healing stage by itself," she reminded the two men at the end of her story. "It was a combination of peroxide, endless permanganate soakings, and constant exercise in the gulf waters that kept the wound open and washed clean. Jody has spent at least half his waking hours walking in the water, moving around to help heal that wound. He's down to three hours a day now."

She looked over at Mr. Tanner thoughtfully. "Jody has a long way to go before he will be ready for school or anything else. He still needs this kind of therapy. He's doing fine right where he is."

The light from the living room shone dimly into Jody's bedroom, where he stood combing his hair in front of a mirror. He had dried his tears and now, listening to Miss Taffy's voice coming from the other room, he felt his courage returning. He reached for his crutch and made his way out into the lighted room.

"Don't sit down just yet, Jody," Taffy said, giving the boy a quick glance. "Let me pull up a chair next to Mr. Tanner and your uncle. I want you to take your bandage off."

Jody obliged with a sidelong look at her. He eased into the chair she set for him and, propping his injured leg on another chair, slowly began to unwind the bandage. When the last fold fell away, exposing the open wound, John Hillard's face turned pale. Mr. Tanner whistled softly under his breath.

"The catfish fin broke off, Mr. Tanner," Jody volunteered calmly, not looking at his uncle. "It took all this time to work out."

Jeff came out of the kitchen with the coffee. After placing the mugs on the table, he spoke to the two men. "I don't mean to butt in on this"—he nodded first at John, then at Mr. Tanner—"but I'd like to say something, if I may."

Mr. Tanner turned to look at Jeff. "Of course, son."

Jeff pulled out a chair and sat down. "You've heard quite a lot from Taffy about how I've helped these two over some rough spots, but she's said nothing about what they've done for me. To put it simply, when I came out here to the island, I was as discouraged and down and out as they were."

In a relaxed manner, Jeff talked about the unemployment situation he had been up against in Tampa, along with his unsuccessful attempts to find work in St. Clair. "I was down to my last cup of grits when I came across these two holed up in the lagoon."

Jody's eyes opened wide when he heard this.

"That day turned out to be a turning point in all our lives." Jeff talked about his ignorance of making a living from the water. "About all I knew how to do was row a boat," he said, "but these two pros"—he grinned over at Jody and Taffy—"took me in hand and made a real fisherman out of me in nothing flat." He told about his daily trips into St. Clair to sell the fish they caught, the way the proceeds were handled for groceries and medicine, and the three-way split of the money left over each week.

"For the first time in my life, I was making a decent living—enough to send money home to my folks in Tampa and still have some left over. Jody and Taffy have saved money, too. As a matter of fact"—Jeff spread his hands to emphasize the importance of his statement—"not long ago I heard Jody say he had ninety dollars stashed away in a jar in his room."

John couldn't keep from smiling with pride when he heard this bit of news. Mr. Tanner's eyes shone. "Ninety dollars? Incredible!"

Jeff went on, speaking to John. "Like Taffy said, sir, Jody is happy here. The island has been good to us, but especially to Jody."

All eyes were trained on Jeff's face. When it became apparent that no one was going to comment, he continued, speaking in his unhurried southern drawl. He chose his next words very carefully.

"I feel the same way Taffy does, sir. As you saw a few

minutes ago, Jody still needs therapy, and with your permission, sir, he's welcome to stay here with me as long as he wishes. There's a school over in St. Clair, from first through eighth grade. When Jody is well enough to attend, when he no longer needs a crutch to get around or the permanganate soakings, I'll personally see that he attends regularly. I'll row him over there myself each morning and fetch him back home when school is out. I'll see that he keeps up his grades, provide for his expenses during the school terms, and see that he's well fed.

"This is not an act of charity, sir. I owe it to Jody. I owe it to him for all the patience and invaluable knowledge he's passed on to me since I've been here. Had it not been for him, and Taffy, I'd still be looking for a job."

Still speaking to John, Jeff added quietly, "All during the time I've known your nephew, sir, I've never once heard him complain about the pain or the inconvenience of his handicap. I think what got him most of all was the fact that he couldn't go trout fishing in the sound with Taffy and me. He couldn't tolerate weight on his leg. Even so, many times when we got back, we would find he had managed to bring in a fair amount of salable fish simply by throwing out his line. He went about the jobs he *could* handle, regardless of what they were, with open-minded cheerfulness. I have respect for the boy and have enjoyed his company since the day we met in the lagoon. I've come to regard him as a little brother."

A note of appeal softened Jeff's voice."I'll take good care of the boy, sir, . . . with your permission, of course."

Jody, unprepared for Jeff's unconditional support, sat stunned as his friend's words struck home. His body tingled with new excitement. He glanced cautiously at Mr. Tanner, then at Taffy. The old man was looking at Jeff, a strange light playing in his eyes. Taffy squeezed Jody's hand reassuringly under the table.

Mr. Tanner took the pipe out of his mouth and slid it into the ashtray. He cleared his throat, looking uneasily at John, who nervously fingered his coffee mug, looking at no one in particular. John was fully aware that he had lost his nephew. He knew that if he ever expected to win back the boy's confidence, he would have to work at it. It was something that would take time—a lot of time— but, somewhere in the future, perhaps Jody would be his friend again. For now, that hope was all he had to go on. It would have to be enough.

He sighed heavily. So engrossed was he in his own thoughts, he failed to notice Mr. Tanner's close scrutiny. When he felt a warm hand on his shoulder, he looked up in surprise.

"Been doing some thinking, John," Mr. Tanner said gently. "Doesn't seem right somehow to be dragging this boy away from a place like this, with him making money, and a school over there in St. Clair, and this young man"—he gestured in Jeff's direction—"who has so graciously offered to look after him."

He hurried on before John could respond. "Besides, from the looks of your nephew's leg, I can't help but agree with Taffy and Jeff. He needs the therapy he's getting here to help the healing process. What do you think, John?"

A resigned smile settled over John's face. "I think you're right, sir," he answered.

With that, he turned to his nephew, whose eyes glistened as he stared at his uncle. "Whether you believe me or not, Jody, I *do* love you and always will. Above all else, I'm going to hang on to the hope that someday you can find it in your heart to forgive this stupid old uncle of yours, and we can be friends again."

John turned away so his nephew wouldn't see the tears that suddenly stung his eyes. He settled farther down in his chair, confident that he had just taken a step in the right direction. He had given his nephew the freedom he wanted—surely the boy would feel a little kinder toward him for it.

Before his voice broke up, John turned to Jeff. "I'm mighty grateful to you, son. You're a good man."

Mr. Tanner broke the silence that followed. "What kind of fishing have you three been doing out here?" he asked Jeff.

Jeff smiled, teeth flashing in his tanned face. He was glad to change the subject and talked about the hook-and-line fishing in the sound, the groupers and redfish in the pass at night, and the pompano at the south pass. "We can bring in flounder or mangrove snapper or even kingfish or cobias just about anytime we want to throw a line off the dock. Fishing is good, and the money keeps coming in."

The old man mulled this over. John, too, had reported good fishing on his way north from Boca Grande Pass. And he'd had a lively discussion with that fish dealer over in St. Clair. A man could do a lot more that just make ends meet by fishing these virgin waters. Mr. Fulton had even hinted that he might take in a partner, if he could find the right person—one with a little working capital to get started, one who might help bring new blood into the fishing business.

"This homestead property of your grandfather's," Mr. Tanner said to Jeff, "how much of it does your father still own?"

"All of it, sir. Three hundred and twenty acres on the north point here, from gulf to bay."

"Think your father might be of a mind to lease some of it?"

The question caught Jeff off guard. Most of the evening had had to do with the problems of Jody and his uncle. Now, out of the blue, the old man was talking about a land lease!

"A land lease, sir? I feel sure he would consider it. Why do you ask?"

Mr. Tanner fiddled with his pipe again. He packed it with fresh tobacco and put a match to the bowl. "Well, seems like everybody I come in contact with—you, John, and that Mr. Fulton over there in St. Clair—is talking about good fishing around these parts. I'm beginning to get down to some serious thought. Like leasing some land here on the bay side and putting up another fish house. Bringing up some of my own crew."

Jeff felt sudden excitement as the old man's proposal began to take form in his mind. A fish house right here on his island! Storage any time of the day or night. A working arrangement with Mr. Fulton. Money for his dad from the lease.

Another hush fell over the house as each one in the room became immersed in his own thoughts, all different.

John, too, was excited. Although Mr. Tanner's plans had come as no surprise to him, hearing him put them into words suddenly brought new hope. He could see a new life opening up for him. Mr. Tanner would help him get a fresh start. Maybe he would build a cabin on the island. . . .

Jody felt wound up like a tight spring. He got out of his chair and, picking up his crutch, headed for the kitchen for no reason other than to let off steam. He reappeared with some of Miss Taffy's oatmeal cookies. Had it really been only a few minutes ago that he was fighting a losing battle, defeat staring him in the face at every turn? He was *free!* Free to stay on his beloved island for the rest of his life if he wanted to. Free to live in this house with Miss Taffy and Jeff.

Taffy felt relieved over Jody's arrangement with his uncle, and now, as her ice blue eyes followed him about, a lump came into her throat. She felt an inner peace and a deep sense of pride. She would never doubt Jody's ability to handle himself in a tight situation again—not after the way he had stood up to his Uncle John *and* Mr. Tanner.

As for Jeff, Taffy had expected all along that he would come through with an appeal in Jody's behalf, but the business about the school in St. Clair? The red carpet he had rolled out for the boy? And the eloquent manner in which he had presented it all? In just two short hours her world had been completely turned around. So many questions had been answered! She would stay on the island with Jody and Jeff, and, when Jody was in shape to go back to school, she could finish her own education at the high school in Twin Oaks.

Was it only a few months ago she had felt, with her grandfather gone, that she was completely alone in the world? She looked fondly at Jody. And she looked at Jeff, who had become the best friend she ever had. She knew she could count on him to keep things going while she and Jody were in school. He would always be there when he was needed. And Mr. Tanner. How nice to have him back in her life again.

She might even go back to Buttonwood Harbor—to see Reverend Hammond again . . . to walk up the gangplank of her grandfather's shack once more . . . to bury her face in the bunt of his unfinished cast net, where his hands had worked so patiently. She could bring it back here to Jody to finish.

She remembered the silent prayer she had said at her grandfather's funeral. "Please, God, let him have a small place by the sea. . . ."

By the sea . . .

Had God heard her earnest appeal?

The thought passed through her with a comforting warmth.

By the sea . . .

The beautiful sea was all around her.